Cyberpunk City
Book Two
Anarchy Boyz

D.L. Young

Cover art by Ignacio Bazan-Lazcano

For free books, new release updates, exclusive previews and content, visit dlyoungfiction.com

I need to do things on my own, need to be left alone.

— Henry Rollins

1
THE UNFORTUNATE MR. SANCHEZ

All hell broke loose in virtual space. Of course it did, Maddox reflected. He'd been warned as much, hadn't he? That twist in his stomach, that annoying tickle in the back of his mind, that something's-not-right-here feeling. They had all told him something was going to go sideways on this particular gig. But he'd convinced himself the meat was unreliable, that sometimes it overreacted, gave you false alarms. And it did, from time to time.

Just not this time.

"That's it," the company man had said a minute earlier. He'd stopped his avatar ten clicks short of Takaki-Chen Engineering's datasphere, its virtualized digital infrastructure.

A neat cluster of geometric shapes, T-Chen Engineering's DS was exactly the kind of digital architecture you'd expect from a company full of engineers. No wasted space, no superfluous connections. All order, zero chaos. The company's departments visualized as brilliantly illuminated towering rectangular partitions, like buildings in a city center, alive and pulsing with uncountable bytes of information.

"Which one's Logistics?" Maddox asked.

"Pale blue," the company man answered. "Small department on the far left, shaped like a brick."

The company man's name was Sanchez, and his story was one Maddox had heard a hundred times. A disgruntled employee—pissed off at being passed over for a promotion or receiving a less-than-expected salary bump or getting nudged out of the inner circle of company movers and shakers (Maddox suspected Sanchez fell into this last category)—decided to take matters into his own hands and sell company secrets to the highest bidder. The only problem was he didn't have any criminal knowhow. So while the company man had easy access to valuable company data, he didn't have the first clue how to: one, steal said data without getting caught; two, sell it on the black market; and, three, hide the proceeds from his employer, the police, the tax man, and—if he fit the profile of most corporati—his wife and his mistress too.

That's where Blackburn Maddox came in, filling a niche in the market. Providing supply where there was demand for a specialist in the acquisition and commercialization of illicit digital assets. For a datajacker, in other words.

"After you," Maddox said.

The glowing orb of Sanchez's avatar lurched forward. The clumsy movement betrayed Sanchez as a lightweight, as someone with little experience in core-level virtual space. Your average citizen never went this deep, experiencing VS at its standard harmless level through their specs. For the vast majority, VS meant gaming, shopping, movies, business meetings, tourist overlay maps, and so on.

Core-level VS was entirely different. A treacherous sea compared to a backyard pool.

A visual representation of the cybernetic world, core-level VS was the real-time three-dimensional skeleton of the interconnected dataspheres and archives making up the digital universe. Core VS was a blueprint, the plumbing behind the walls, the giant machine's hidden circuitry, rarely witnessed or experienced by the average user. To get there you needed specialized high-end hardware: a VS data deck and an electrode headset like the kind plugged into Maddox's meat back in his office.

It also helped if you were a bit insane. Or if not insane, at least capable of coping with the lethal threat core VS posed. Everyday VS, the variety ninety-nine point nine percent of the global population experienced, interacted with the brain only at a very superficial, harmless level via the tiny built-in brain wave sensors embedded in the temple arms of nearly every pair of specs. This was a light touch from a gloved hand compared to the choke grip of core VS, which penetrated the human brain to its deepest neural pathways, taxing its processing capability to the maximum. Brain scans of datajackers inside core VS, Maddox had once heard, lit up like a neon sign cranked to max brightness. And therein lay the danger. At the virtualized depths where Maddox and others in his field practiced their trade, you were vulnerable, your nervous system was open to any number of attacks. Your avatar could be frozen by countermeasures in nanoseconds that paralyzed your real-world meat sack like it was stuck in concrete. You could be geotagged by programs that traced your physical location. Some of the rarer, more powerful and generally illegal apps and executables—ones Maddox had some familiarity with—could alter your perception of time, turning real-world minutes into virtual hours and days, even months. Others, the worst kind, induced fatal brain strokes.

Such were the hazards of his chosen profession. Every career had its downside, he sometimes told himself. But fuck if he didn't love it.

His avatar fell in behind Sanchez, and Maddox warily scanned the space around them for any hint they'd been detected. No alarms blared, no intelligent sentries came after them, no countermeasures were tripped. The cloaking app was doing its job. Maddox and Sanchez were all but invisible to everything but each other.

As they approached T-Chen Engineering's logistics partition, Maddox's field of vision filled with the blue glow of the partition's incandescence. Sanchez stopped one click short. The department loomed over them like some brilliant neon midrise.

"It's around the other side," Sanchez said. Maddox followed as the company man's avatar slid along the face of the partition until it reached the rearmost corner. The partition's surface swirled and churned ominously, the telltale visualization of a razorwall, the security application protecting the department's digital assets—its archives and communications and vital records. Beyond the wall's opaque, shifting surface, company data surged and pulsed, shooting up and down and back and forth in brilliant streams of yellow and orange and white. A busy department going about its daily routine of meetings and reports and smoke breaks and office gossip. It was a world Maddox had been a part of for a brief time, working as a data security analyst at Latour-Fisher Biotechnologies. The legit world. The comfortable, insulated world of those who followed the rules, who never doubted the hierarchy, who fretted day and night over their careers and connections. It wasn't a world for someone like him, as it turned out. A square peg, round hole situation, but the regular paycheck hadn't been too bad.

"There it is." Sanchez indicated a small dull gray box hovering just inside the wall. Exactly where the company man said he'd stashed it. The box was the visualization of an archive, inside of which Sanchez had hidden the company's three-year mergers and acquisitions plan. Information competitors would pay a small fortune for.

That was when the knot formed itself in Maddox's stomach. Even though his body was a distant sensation, he still felt it. Something wasn't right. Maybe it was the client, maybe it was the plan, or maybe it was the weird vibe the razorwall was giving him. But whatever it was, the meat was trying to tell him something.

"You sure that's it?" Maddox asked.

"I'm sure."

"Stay right here," he told the man. "Don't move. Not even a single grid click, yeah?"

"Yes, yes," Sanchez said. "Got it." Maddox heard the nervousness, the excitement in the man's voice. Wherever it was the company man's meat sack was sitting at the moment, his palms had to be damp with sweat.

"You're sure these cloaking apps are working

right?" Sanchez asked.

"They're fine," Maddox assured him. "If they weren't working, we'd be deaf and blind from all the alarms going off right about now."

Maddox edged forward. "I'm going in," he said, his tone confident. The rest of him, not so much. Back in his office, Maddox's hands gestured, and inside VS a scanning app appeared in the lower part of his vision.

Maddox moved forward and penetrated the razorwall. He felt an abrupt tingling sensation, like he'd stepped through a waterfall of freezing water. In the next moment he was through. No alarms sounded, no countermeasures appeared. Nothing on the scanner. So far so good, but he still felt a stab of doubt.

Around him data pulsed and surged, immeasurable bytes of visualized information shooting left and right, down and up, bright and dazzling like the birth of some universe. Settling himself, he reacquired the target archive, opened it, and began emptying its contents into his avatar's temp storage, a thief filling his bag with a jewelry store's diamonds and gems. The box slowly dissolved and then after a few moments disappeared, signifying the end of the data dump.

He pushed back through the razorwall, exiting the department. As he did so, he heard Sanchez let out a long breath.

"All right," Maddox said. "Let's get out of here."

Blink. The company man's avatar glitched, winking like a failing lightbulb. Maddox backed his avatar away.

What do you know, the meat was right.

"What…happening…?" Sanchez's voice clipped

and cut out.

Maddox glanced down at the scanner and quickly gathered what had happened. He hadn't tripped any alarms himself. The razorwall status was green and there were no signs of intrusion from inside the departmental partition. It was Sanchez. An intelligent sentry had detected him.

It happened sometimes. A function of bad luck. A wrong place at the wrong time kind of thing. Intelligent sentries were like beat cops patrolling a datasphere, programmed to look for any number of things: inefficiencies in data flows, vulnerabilities in razorwalls, legacy apps left lying around like discarded food wrappers that needed scrapping or archiving. They also kept an eye out for signs of unauthorized access, for illegal infiltrators like Sanchez and Maddox.

Normally, Maddox's settings would have revealed an IS's presence. They typically visualized as crablike creatures crawling across the virtual surfaces of departmental partitions, and they were pretty easy to avoid. You simply kept a safe distance. But this one was invisible to him, which told Maddox it was a high-end IS or one that had been tweaked by someone who really knew what they were doing.

The curious engineer in him wanted to learn more, to take a few scans and diagnostics of the thing, but the sensible side of him knew he didn't have time. Not if he wanted to keep from being frozen like the unfortunate Mr. Sanchez, who right about now was probably flipping out, wondering why he couldn't move his arms and legs. Or maybe he'd gotten past the initial panic, realizing what was happening, knowing that while he was frozen, the IS was also geotagging him and alerting the authorities. In a handful of minutes, it would all be over. Cops would break down the door to his home or office or rented hotel suite or wherever Sanchez had holed up to steal his company's secrets, then they'd shock him unconscious and drag him off to jail. It was the fate every datajacker dreaded and feared. And if he stayed around any longer, Maddox knew the sentry would see him too, freeze him, and that would be that.

So he bailed, dumping the stolen data from his temp storage and unplugging.

And then he was back in the meat. Back in his tiny rented room. Disconnected and safe, unlike the unfortunate Mr. Sanchez.

He peeled off the trodes, plastic cups popping from the skin of his forehead, and sat up in his eggshell recliner. A standby icon slowly rotated in the air a few centimeters above his deck, held firmly by the docking arm. The arm adjusted its position as Maddox sat up further, keeping the deck within easy reach.

He swung his legs around and stood up, sliding his hand through the standby icon and shutting down the deck. A cigarette. Christ, he needed a cigarette.

*   *   *

Beyond his narrow jut of a balcony where Maddox had barely enough space for himself and a folding chair, the nighttime City churned. Twenty stories below, ground cars congested East Harlem's arteries, klaxon echoes and the infrequent wails of sirens rising to his ears from the City's floor. Walkways teemed with pedestrians, a river of humanity pulsing with the reflected glare of giant holo ads projected onto building facades. At Maddox's level, the lower transit lanes bustled with hovers, almost close enough to reach out and touch, moving among the massive superstructures of steel and concrete. The pitch of turbofan motors rose and fell as vehicles came and went.

He blew smoke out into the open air, pondering Sanchez's fate. The company man was probably sitting in an interrogation room right about now, sweating hard and trying to convince some hardened cop this was all some misunderstanding. The cop would ask who he'd been working with, but Sanchez had nothing more than one of the dozens of aliases Maddox worked under. Once the police learned where the two had met (an anonymous chat feed with untraceable hard encryption) and how well they were acquainted (not very, they'd never met in person), they wouldn't bother trying to find the company man's accomplice, knowing it was a waste of time, knowing from experience there'd be no trail to follow.

Leaving a client high and dry, he admitted inwardly, wasn't exactly the pinnacle of professional behavior. It was, in fact, the kind of thing that could seriously damage your rep if it got out. In the small world of high-end datajacking, rep mattered. Not so much with a little fish like Sanchez, but it mattered to the big players, the highfloor corporati who on occasion hired datajackers for big money corporate espionage jobs and who stayed current on the black market reps the same way a pro football scout keeps up with teenage talent in South America. It also mattered inside the tiny club of vain, jealous, ego-driven elite datajackers who often savored a rival's failure. And in those moments when he thought about it—those rare instances of self-reflection—he knew it mattered to him, too. He was a data thief. He liked it. Loved it, even. And he took selfish pride in it. Call it ego, narcissism, whatever.

The debacle with Sanchez wouldn't get out, he was sure. It was a small gig for a midlevel corporati. A nothing job for a nobody, and since no money had changed hands—Maddox had agreed to a contingency deal, his cut paid when the stolen goods were sold—there was little to worry about. He'd even dumped the goods out of caution, washing his hands of the whole business.

Even before it had blown up on him, he hadn't liked the job from the start. It was nothing he could put his finger on. Not the client, Sanchez, not the target company, Takaki-Chen Engineering, not the nature of the gig itself. Still, something hadn't felt right about it.

Which was why he'd cut a hole in Sanchez's cloak. It was a cover-your-ass move, the kind of maneuver most datajackers did from time to time but would never admit to. You compromised the security of your client's avatar or connection, just the tiniest bit, removing a single line of crucial code in a cloaking app, for instance. And if the proverbial shit hit the fan during the gig, the countermeasures or intelligent sentinels or whatever other digital security was in place would detect the client first, leaving you a few precious moments to safely unplug. It was a bit like tripping your bankrobbing accomplice as the cops chased you both down an alley. Underhanded, yes. Douchey, most certainly. But it was an effective way to keep yourself out of jail when you had a sketchy client or a job you had reservations about.

A part of Maddox felt for the guy. He knew firsthand that corporate types weren't cut out for jail cells with shit-stained mattresses, much less the lowfloor brutality of police shocksticks and long, torturous interrogations.

But the thought was a fleeting one, snuffed out by the rigid, cold practicality required by his profession. If somebody had to take the fall, it wasn't going to be him.

Sorry, Mr. Sanchez.

2
NATURAL JACK

The ring announcer's voice didn't match his body. He was a small, thin man, well into his seventies, and the microphone trembled visibly in his gnarled, arthritic hands. The voice, though. It boomed over the PA system with the strength and clarity of an opera singer in his prime.

"LADIES AND GENTLEMEN, I GIVE YOU SHINJI THE SAMURAI NAGANO...NAGANO." The announcer always repeated the fighter's last name. His signature flair.

The raucous crowd roared when the first fighter entered the makeshift arena. More boos than cheers, Maddox noted. He took a long drink of his beer as the house lights went down and a spotlight appeared near the back of the crowd. Samurai Nagano, a sumo-sized giant with arms as big around as Maddox's thighs, raised his arms to the noisy throng. Dressed in black ninja gear, he held a pair of blades, which gleamed in the spotlight's glare as he crossed them over his head. The boos and cheers grew louder. Nagano knew how to work a room.

Maddox didn't come to the underground fights often. The venue was always some crumbling warehouse in one of the sketchier parts of town. The beer was always watered down, and the crowd…well, it wasn't exactly his crowd. Loud and drunk and lusty for violence. It wasn't uncommon for more fights to break out in the audience than were scheduled on the card. He could think of twenty better ways to spend his evening, but he'd been dodging the invitation for weeks and he'd run out of excuses. He stood away from the crowd, near an exit at the rear of the venue with his back to the wall. He took another drink of what passed for beer. Discarded plastic cups and cigarette butts littered the floor.

The datajacker's thoughts returned briefly to his disastrous run in virtual space earlier that day. Next time he'd pay more attention to his gut, he promised himself.

He'd made it out in one piece, though, untagged and unfrozen. No small thing, that, and the clean getaway reminded him of the biggest advantage to running a one-man shop: things were a lot easier when the only ass you had to worry about was your own. Sure, there were jobs you had to pass up on if you didn't have a trained crew to help out. Huge gigs, the complex ones where you needed a dozen jackers hitting the same datasphere at the same time, each with a specific assignment. Still, for Maddox the upsides of working alone far outweighed the downsides. Everything began and ended with you. You didn't have to train some green kid, didn't have to share money with a partner. And if you screwed up, it was your mess to deal with and yours alone. With the lone exception of today's debacle with

Sanchez, his solo venture had been working out pretty well over these last months. A one-man shop, while admittedly less lucrative than a bigger operation, seemed to be a perfect fit for him.

The spotlight followed Nagano as the fighter plodded his way to the ring, surrounded by security who cut a path for him through the sea of bodies. Hands reached for him, touching his back and shoulders. Beer sprayed through the air, thrown in the fighter's direction. By the time he climbed into the ring, his ninja suit was spotted all over with beer stains. His assistants took his blades, then slowly removed his mask as the crowd jeered. Next the top and bottom garments came off, leaving the barefisted, barefooted fighter clothed only in his sparring shorts. The man was heavily modded. Maddox could see that even from a distance.

"AND HIS OPPONENT…"

Maddox winced as the crowd erupted into a deafening roar, drowning out the announcer's introduction. The old man, pro that he was, compensated for the noise, shouting into the mic and holding it flush to his lips as he rattled off the opponent's height and weight and win-loss record.

"LADIES AND GENTLEMEN, I GIVE YOU NATURAL JACK KADREY…KADREY."

The spotlight zipped across the venue, skimming over a blur of tightly packed bodies and stopping at a doorway a few meters from Maddox. In the doorway stood the second fighter. Natural Jack, all two meters and a hundred thirty muscled kilos of him. Dark-skinned and hairless except for a round tuft of dyed yellow hair atop his head, he cut a mean silhouette in the spotlight's white glare. The crowd went wild at the sight of him. The hero had arrived. With his hands on his hips, Jack lifted his chin to the crowd and sneered. Impossibly, the roar of the crowd intensified.

Jack started toward the ring, his eyes fixed on his opponent. A steely glare, full of bad intentions. Just before he disappeared into the crowd, surrounded by his entourage, he glanced over at Maddox. The fighter's death stare instantly disappeared, and he gave his old friend a wink and a grin. The look of a naughty kid who loved nothing more than behaving badly. Maddox returned the gesture with a slow, exaggerated clap.

After prefight introductions that would probably last longer than the fight itself, the referee explained the rules to the spectators. A tiny man with a pencil mustache, Maddox couldn't imagine how the ref would manage to handle these two enormous men. The recounting of the rules didn't take long because, essentially, there weren't any. All strikes were legal and no areas of the body were off-limits. No rounds, no stopping until it was over. The first man who tapped out or (in the event he was unconscious) whose corner threw in the towel was the loser. Above the ring, a trio of cam drones fluttered like dragonflies, broadcasting the fight on the underground feeds.

The bell rang and the fighters circled each other, cautiously feeling out one another's defenses with quick long-range jabs and kicks. Maddox watched, smoking anxiously. Jack had always been able to handle himself inside the ring. Still, the palpable violence in the air, the feeling of the crowd's barely contained madness, permeated the venue and unnerved Maddox.

A few minutes in, both men started landing blows. Hard ones. The kind you could hear in the small moments when the crowd noise lessened. A meaty thud followed by gasps and oohs from the crowd. Jack began to tire, Maddox noticed. He'd opened the fight dancing on the balls of his feet, improbably spry for such a large man. But now, fifteen minutes in, he was flat-footed and sluggish. Nagano was still fresh. Impossibly so, Maddox thought. He had to have something pumping through his veins. Nanobots maxing his blood oxygen. Synthetic adrenaline, maybe.

Three brutal one-sided minutes later, Jack finally went down. A right cross on the point of his chin dropped him onto his back, and he lay there motionless, his arms spread out wide. A white towel flew out of his corner and landed on his chest. Nagano leaned over his fallen opponent, screaming at him in Japanese, gesturing wildly for Jack to get up so he could beat him down a second time. The ref stepped in front of him and waved his arms overhead and that was that. The fight was over.

Nagano's cornermen rushed into the ring, joyfully stomping and flailing their arms. They hoisted their man onto their shoulders. The crowd booed and jeered and hurled hundreds of plastic cups into the ring. Through the swirling chaos of shouts and raised fists and flying beer cups, Maddox caught a glimpse of Jack being helped out of the ring by his trainers. A cam drone fluttered above the vanquished fighter's head, broadcasting his walk of shame back to the dressing room.

*   *   *

"You weren't exactly my good luck charm tonight,

were you, Blackburn?" Jack grinned at Maddox. The fighter's teeth were discolored from blood and his right eye was swollen half-shut. Shirtless and still in his fighting shorts, he sat on a folding chair in the tiny dressing room, his hands plunged into a bucket of ice water. His cut man hovered around him, carefully tending to Jack's multiple scrapes and bruises. The muffled sounds of the emcee's amplified voice and the crowd seeped through the walls. The next fight was about to start.

"You'll live," the cut man said, rubbing the top of his head like a doting mother.

"No stitches?" Jack asked.

The cut man shook his head.

"Good," Jack said, glancing at Maddox again with his mischievous grin. "Can't scar up this pretty face. Ladies prefer a man with smooth skin, you know."

Maddox lit a cigarette. "You always take getting your ass kicked this well?"

Jack shrugged. "Win some, lose some. Such is life."

"You can't smoke in here," the cut man said sharply.

Jack raised a wet hand out of the bucket, waiving the man off. "It's all right, Angelo."

The cut man gave Maddox a disapproving look, then left the two men alone, shutting the door behind him.

Jack removed his other hand from the ice bucket. "Ah." He grimaced, massaging his knuckles. Water ran down his forearms, dripping from his elbows onto the floor. "Cold, cold, cold. Nothing works better for the swelling, though."

Maddox threw him a towel. "Thanks," the fighter

said, drying his hands. "So how's things?"

"Not bad," Maddox said. "Had a bit of a bust today, but in general, can't complain."

Jack tilted his head. "Back on top again, are we?"

"Getting there."

The fighter tossed the towel at Maddox's chest, grinned. "That's not what I hear. The street says you're tearing it up. Kicking all kinds of ass." Jack stood slowly, groaning as he rose. He moved to the small mirror on the wall and examined himself, pivoting his chin back and forth. He gingerly put a finger to his swollen eye. "It's good you're in the game again, doing well. Makes my soul sing, seeing you back in the mix." He turned and looked at Maddox. "You got a lady friend?"

Maddox blew smoke. "It's been mostly work lately."

Jack shot him a disappointed look. "O, how full of briers is this working-day world."

"*Merchant of Venice*?" Maddox asked. Ever since he'd known Jack, the fighter had made a habit of quoting Shakespeare. Maddox didn't know the works very well, and he rarely placed the lines to the correct play.

"*As You Like It*," Jack said, then turned the subject back to Maddox. "So all work and no play, is it?"

"More or less."

The fighter turned on the tap in the small sink, leaned down, splashed water on his face. "You need to get some joy in your life." He crossed the room, turned the chair backwards, and sat in front of Maddox. Beads of water ran down his forehead, dripped from his chin.

"You got to get out more, my brother."

Maddox smoked. "Did it ever occur to you that if you went out less and trained a bit more, you wouldn't have just gotten KO'd?"

Jack furrowed his brow in mock indignation. "That's cold." He took Maddox's cigarette, inhaled a deep drag, then handed it back. "You're a cold-blooded man, Blackburn Maddox." He blew smoke. "I invite you down here, get you free admission, a backstage pass. Now you're going to make me go home and cry myself to sleep."

Maddox finally cracked a smile. He was glad he had come. It was good to see an old friend. Jack was one of the few who hadn't abandoned him, who hadn't blamed him for what had happened with Rooney.

The fighter stood up. "Come on," he said, smiling broadly again, "let's go out and tear it up. I'm buying." He toweled off his naked torso, arm and chest muscles rippling.

"Go out?" Maddox said. "You've got to be kidding me."

The fighter lowered his chin, lifted his eyebrows. "Did you really say that?"

"You just got knocked out."

The fighter removed the cigarette from Maddox's mouth, took a puff, then gave it back. "And your point is?"

Maddox smiled inwardly. Of course they were going out. This was Natural Jack Kadrey. The ladies' man. The man's man. The walking party.

"Sure," he said. "We'll celebrate your loss."

Jack clapped his hands. "That's what I'm talking about." There was a knock on the door. Jack opened it. Samurai Nagano in the doorway.

"Come on in, Shinji," Jack said.

Nagano entered, wearing flip-flops, baggy shorts, and a white T-shirt dotted with wet spots. His hair was damp and a towel hung around his neck. "Good showers here, Jack. Water's nice and warm." Nagano noticed Maddox, then lifted his eyebrows at Jack.

"He's fine," Jack said. "One of my turfies. We go way back."

Jack put his hand on Nagano's shoulder, examined the damage to his opponent's left eye. "That's gonna be a nice shiner tomorrow. Need any pain pills?"

"Thanks, I'm good," Nagano answered. He rubbed the towel against his hair. "Listen, I just wanted to…" He looked over to Maddox again.

Jack laughed. "He's fine, I'm telling you. No secrets between us. I vouch for him."

This seemed to put Nagano at ease. He reached into his pocket, removed a roll of cash as thick around as his forearm. "Just wanted to say thanks," he said, holding out the money. Nagano's head was down, his voice was quiet and respectful, almost apologetic.

"Unnecessary, my friend," Jack said, shaking his head, waving the money away. "Give that beautiful little girl of yours a kiss for me."

Nagano slowly pocketed the bills, then his face twisted and he took in a quick breath, as if he were trying to block a sudden surge of emotion. He reached out and hugged Jack, gripping the man tightly to him. Jack laughed in surprise and returned the embrace. "She'll be just fine, Shinji. You'll see. Just fine."

Nagano finally let go, his face streaked with tears. He thanked Jack again, bowing repeatedly, then turned and left. Jack stood there, staring at the door for a few moments.

"You filthy cheat," Maddox said. "You took a dive?"

Jack grabbed his shirt and pulled it over his head. "Imagine that," he said. "Something shady going on in the world of illegal fighting. What's the world coming to?"

"Bookies don't look kindly on that kind of thing, you know. Word gets out and there goes your career. It's no joke, Jack."

"I'll tell you what's no joke," Jack said, suddenly serious. He gestured toward the door. "It wasn't no joke when they found cancer in Shinji's daughter. And it wasn't no joke when those medical bills started piling up. And it sure as hell wasn't no joke when they stopped treatment because Shinji couldn't pay." Jack shook his head, disgusted. "You ought to see that little girl, Blackburn. Bright eyes, big old smile that'll break your heart right in two."

"So you two planned all this out and then bet on your knockout."

Jack winked. "You always could put two and two together."

"So who placed the bet?"

"Some corporati Shinji used to give judo lessons." He smiled. "Bookies had Shinji a ten-to-one underdog."

"Not a bad payday," Maddox said.

"Not bad at all."

Maddox smoked. "And so the undefeated record goes out the window."

The fighter looked in the mirror, patted his face dry with the towel. He gazed at his own face, then shifted his eyes to Maddox and shrugged. "Way I see it, there's losing and then there's losing." He rubbed the towel over the top of his head. "You see the look on Shinji's face? Hell, that's not losing. That's just about the farthest thing from it, brother."

The fighter tossed the towel to the floor, swiveled around to Maddox, then snapped his fingers and shimmied his shoulders to some dance music playing in his head. "All right, datajacker, you ready to hit the town with this loser?"

*   *   *

Around 2 a.m., Maddox finally managed to slip away unnoticed from the party, which by then had grown to encompass every patron in the club. Natural Jack Kadrey was a people magnet. Handsome (even with the swollen eye) and charming and famous in an underground sort of way, people were drawn to him like moths to a flame. Maddox left Jack in high spirits, his hands wrapped around the waists of two beautiful women on his lap, whispering to them in turn, making plans for later.

Maddox lit a cigarette and headed down Sixth Avenue. The City churned around him, ever wakeful, ever alive. The walkways were congested, as usual, a state that never changed or even seemed to lessen, no matter what the hour of day or night. The streets were just as clogged as the walkways. Ground cars snailed their way along at a pace only slightly better than the thick flow of pedestrian traffic. In his specs, a carousel of ads and street vendor barks rotated in the lower left of his vision, the portion of his lenses reserved as commercial real estate.

FIVE STAR TACOS DE CHORIZO NEXT LEFT!

DO YOU KNOW JESUS, FRIEND?
HOLO TATTOOS, BEST IN THE CITY!!!!

Some paid to go ad-free, but blocking tech was expensive and Maddox was tightfisted by nature. Besides, it cost nothing to ignore sales pitches…

BUY ONE BLOW JOB, THE NEXT ONE'S ON US!

…or at least try to ignore them.

He walked on, working off his whiskey buzz, painted in the neon glow of towering holos. Dancing hamburgers. Shoot-'em-up plugin games. A soccer star pimping his signature line of sports clothes. A couple blocks ahead, the Dishi beer anime girl stood twenty stories tall, projected against the face of a standalone condo building. She downed a beer, tilting the mug high as white froth spilled down in rivulets between and around her gravity-defying breasts. She finished and put her hand to her mouth and giggled, then the cycle started over and she lifted the mug again, spilled, and giggled. A line of hovers moved slowly across her face, the automated trudge of the lowest and most crowded of the stacked transit lanes that extended up over a hundred or more stories, each level less crowded than the one underneath it.

As it always did, the City's brightness and noise soothed Maddox. Its crowded walkways of bespectacled strangers offered refuge, peace of mind. Its towering megastructures—the daisy-chained buildings known as hiverises that housed hundreds of thousands, even millions—were timeless, immovable mountain ranges, concrete gods who watched over the City's valley floor. He'd never found the City intimidating or overwhelming as some did. The City was home, its ceaseless throb as natural to him as the beat of his own heart. Sure, you had to keep your wits about you, otherwise trouble would find you, but the street knew who the suckers were, and for the most part it parsed accordingly.

Home was a thirty-story midrise in Tribeca, where Sixth Avenue merged into Church Street. In a previous era it had been a government office building of some kind. Its featureless facade of rust-colored brick and rows of plain rectangular windows shouted twentieth-century public sector austerity. Maddox sometimes wondered what the building had looked like back then, before it had been gradually covered— as most of the City's buildings had—by a rainbow motley of graffiti tags and stencils and freehand pieces. Naked was the word that came to mind. A building with no markups seemed incomplete, unnatural. A mannequin's face with no distinguishing features, fingers without prints. Maddox's favorite graffiti on his home building occupied ten square meters of space just above the entryway, a scene depicting a datajacker in virtual space. Viewed from behind, the jacker sat cross-legged with his arms extended, palms up like some Hindu deity. Floating above one hand was a data visualization, a shiny black cube with COMPANY SECRETS etched on it in red letters. Dollar signs flowed into the other hand, shaped like a funnel cloud of swirling bills. In the background, a trio of corporati in three-piece suits looked on, their faces wide-eyed in horror, hands atop their heads in helpless disbelief as they watched the jacker rob them of their precious IP. Maddox had never been the superstitious sort, but when he'd first seen the piece during his search for a new apartment, a part of him couldn't help but think it was the City's way of telling him 250 Church Street was the right address for his new digs.

"Good evening, Mr. Thornbush," the doorman greeted him, using the fake name Maddox had rented under. The old man politely dipped his chin and touched his hat. His glove was dingy and threadbare, matching the rest of his stained, well-worn uniform. Still, he wore the outfit proudly, with the same professionalism and sense of duty with which he performed his job. The old man seemed perfectly content, even happy, with his place in the universe as the longest-tenured doorman on Church Street.

Maddox smiled and nodded, then paused as the man opened the door for him.

"Cesar, where are your specs?" he asked.

The man looked to the ground, his lined face knotted with uncharacteristic worry. "I'll find them."

"Don't tell me you lost another pair."

"No, no," the man protested, still looking down. "I just misplaced them, that's all. I'll find them, I'm sure of it."

Maddox stood in the doorway. Building gossip had it old Cesar was about to get the boot. He was old and forgetful, and he was always losing his specs, making it impossible for him to call a taxi or perform other services for the building's tenants. There was talk of petitioning the condo board to find a replacement.

Maddox backed out of the doorway and told the old man to close the door. He blinked through his specs' menu, found the factory resets and activated them. A few moments later a confirmation window popped up. He removed the specs and handed them to the old man. He'd never really liked this pair, anyway.

"Here," he said. "I got these free when I bought a timeshare." It wasn't the most believable lie, but it had been a long day and he was tired. He knew the proud old man would never accept anyone's charity.

The doorman looked up at Maddox. "Sir, I can't take your—"

"Give them back when you find your own."

Shaking hands slowly reached out and took the specs. "I will, sir." The man's voice trembled with restrained emotion. "I can't tell you how grateful…" His voice trailed away.

Maddox shifted uncomfortably from one foot to the other. "It's no problem," he said, finally breaking the awkward silence. "Like I said, they were free." He pulled the door open and stepped inside.

Minutes later, he sat on the tiny concrete outcrop of his tenth-story balcony, wearing boxer shorts and smoking. He never liked to sleep when he was whiskey buzzing, and he was still a cigarette or two away from sober. A breeze came off the Hudson River, three blocks to the west beyond the seawall, and cooled his skin. He'd left the TV on in the condo, and the muffled voice of a newsperson came through the glass door. He caught bits and pieces of stories. Something about a terrorist bombing in the financial district, then a corruption scandal in the City's waste removal department, followed by the protests over a proposed cut to the dole, the subsistence income most of the City's jobless residents relied on. Another day in the City.

He blew smoke rings into the air beyond the balcony. They floated away, twisting and folding and losing their shape as they dissipated in the softly pushing breeze. Specs, he reminded himself. He'd have to pick up a new pair in the morning.

3
LEXINGTON AVENUE RAID

"I don't want any upgrades," Maddox repeated, his patience thinning. His head was foggy with too little sleep and the dull throb of a hangover. The vendor, hunched over the specs, hummed in disapproval. He was a little round fellow with a wiry mop of dark hair. Russian, maybe Ukrainian, from his accent. He made small adjustments to the specs' temple arm with a tiny screwdriver. An elastic band around his head held a jeweler's loupe against his left eye.

"I make good deal," he said without looking up from the pair of refurbished Kwan Nouveaus. "Three apps for price of one. You not find better deal anywhere south of the park."

"I've got my own wares," Maddox said firmly.

Again came the hum of disapproval, but at least the man stopped trying to upsell him. Behind the counter, a row of holo displays flickered, rotating through scenes from the street outside. Security cams. Above them, on a larger display, a pair of youths with model good looks argued passionately in Russian. Some serial drama. Maddox only understood bits and pieces—his Russian was sketchy even when he wasn't hungover—but the bad acting needed no translation. The camera zoomed slowly as the argument cooled and the youths drew closer to one another, their disagreement forgotten as they pressed their mouths together in a sudden fit of passion.

"Sorry," the vendor said sheepishly, looking over to the display. He flicked his wrist at the holo, flipping over to a news feed. "My daughter's program," he said, then added, a bit too defensively, "I never watch such silly things."

After a few final tweaks, the man handed Maddox the specs. "You try for fit now."

The specs rested on Maddox's face comfortably. He blinked a sequence, and a config menu appeared, superimposed on the lens. He tested the eyetracking and the blink and subvocalization sensitivity and checked the logs to make sure the pair had been wiped as clean as the vendor had claimed. His eyes flitted and twitched as he rushed through the menus and reset the defaults to his liking.

"You're very fast with eyes," the vendor observed. "You're datajacker, yes?"

"Pastry chef," Maddox said, finishing his checks. He removed the specs, nodded. "These are good."

As he handed the vendor a small stack of bills, something on the news feed caught Maddox's attention. The financial district terrorist bombing. Same story he'd caught a piece of last night on his balcony. BREAKING NEWS scrolled across the display in flashing red letters as the newswoman spoke.

We've got an update on yesterday's bomb attack at Takaki-Chen Engineering's headquarters in the financial district. The death toll now numbers fourteen. A spokesperson for the company said the global firm's employees were shocked and devastated by the senseless act—

"Bah," the vendor said, gesturing the feed away from the story to a soccer match.

"Change it back," Maddox said.

"Why you want to see such terrible things?"

"Change it back!" Maddox barked.

The vendor looked at him sourly, then turned and gestured at the holo. The news feed returned.

…the detonation occurred at four p.m. local time. Police say the bomb was an improvised device, detonated remotely, and they're reviewing public camera footage for suspicious activity.

Maddox swallowed. Four p.m. Takaki-Chen Engineering. He'd been datajacking that very company at that very hour, poking around its digital insides while someone was blowing up its offices in the real world. This was not good, he thought grimly. He turned and left quickly, the bell on the jamb tinkling as he pulled open the door and stepped out onto the noisy, crowded walkway.

Not good at all.

* * *

The zoom on his new specs was good. Even at 50x magnification, the scene outside Maddox's office building was clear and crisp and didn't wobble. He watched from a fifteenth-floor fire escape several blocks away, looking for…he wasn't really sure what for, actually.

The scene in front of the entrance looked like any other weekday morning. Busy, congested, people hurrying the way they only seem to do in the morning. Coffee cups in hand. Long, purposeful strides, destination bound.

Maddox paid a handsome rent for his tiny cramped office in one of the City's nicer domed neighborhoods. Most of his professional counterparts normally worked out of run-down tenements on abandoned streets. The City's empty nooks and crannies, places the police had long since stopped monitoring with cams and drones. But after his stint in the corporate world, Maddox found he could no longer stand such filthy, dilapidated conditions. He'd grown accustomed to a clean, well-lighted working space, so he'd donned the fake identity of a business consultant and rented a small-but-pricey office in the heart of a busy commercial district. The neighborhood also had some of the best noodle joints in the City, which had been an added bonus.

Maddox watched, hoping the sinking feeling he'd had after watching the news feed was nothing. Hoping his datajacking gig and the bombing hitting the same target—on the same day—was just a bad coincidence. A minute later he realized it wasn't.

A dozen police hovers converged on the building, blue and red lights flashing. Two ground cars and a paddy wagon skidded to a stop in front of the entrance. Ten cops clad in full rhino armor poured out of the wagon and hustled into the building, brandishing stubby automatic rifles. The cops in the ground cars jumped out and cleared the walkway in front of the building, damming the flow of pedestrian traffic.

Lifting his view from the street to the tenth floor, Maddox found his office's window. Nothing happened for a long moment as Maddox watched and held his breath. Then a white flash flared and the window shattered outward. In the next instant

Maddox heard the telltale thud of a stun grenade.

He stared in disbelief at the raid on his office. The hovers floated around the building like angry hornets, lights blaring. Through the broken window, he caught glimpses of rhino cops moving through his office.

What the hell was happening?

He blinked up the call menu in his specs and dialed the only person who might be able to tell him.

4
MARKET STREET MEETUP

"Meet you there in half an hour," Maddox said. "And don't forget the gear."

He ended the lens call as he climbed down the last rung of the fire escape. Heading down the alley and turning south on First Avenue, he merged with the flow of foot traffic on the crowded walkway. His mind raced, pulse quickened. He had to calm down, had to think. Removing a cigarette from his pocket case, he lit it and took a slow deep drag. He held it in for a long moment, trying to calm the whirling storm inside his head.

Sanchez. What dirty business had that corporati been mixed up in? He was connected to the bombing. Had to be. The timing was too coincidental.

How had the cops managed to find his office? But more than that, how did they know about him at all? Even if they'd picked up Sanchez and beat a full confession out of him, the client had never known Maddox's name, much less his place of business. Their only meetings had been on two occasions: both in secured, untraceable locations in VS. And for those, Maddox had physically plugged in from a public grid down in the Bowery, a safe distance from his Upper East Side office.

He went over everything again and again, retracing his few dealings with Sanchez, recalling nothing unusual. He'd taken no shortcuts, hadn't said or done anything that might have compromised his anonymity. So, then, how? None of it made any sense.

A bumblebee drone flitted overhead, skimming a few meters above the pedestrians' heads. A tiny glow on its belly alternated red and blue, identifying it as a police drone. Maddox's neck muscles stiffened. He tried not to break stride or make any other suspicious moves the device's motion algorithms would pick up on. He swallowed, kept walking. When the drone buzzed past, ignoring him, Maddox let out a breath. He gave a silent thanks for the one upgrade he'd bought with his new specs—a twenty-pack of stolen IDs that fooled most street cams and police scans. The upgrade had just paid for itself and then some.

Never skimp on wares. It was something Rooney—his late mentor and business partner, a man who'd been famously tightfisted in every other area of his life—had often preached. Top-grade wares could be the difference between getting pinched and walking away. Maddox blew smoke, silently agreeing. True words.

Half an hour later, Maddox found Jack in the abandoned lot where the southernmost end of Market Street dead-ended into the FDR Seawall. Jack wore white-framed specs and sat on an upended crate at the edge of the lot's weedy overgrowth. The seawall loomed large behind the fighter, backdropped by an overcast sky of low gray clouds. As Maddox approached, he noticed the satchel in the fighter's hand.

"Have any problems?" Maddox asked.

Jack shook his head. "Not finding the gear. But this hangover's hitting me harder than Shinji did last night." He smiled. "And I had to kick a couple new friends out of bed earlier than I would have liked to."

"Sorry about that." Maddox took the satchel, looked through it. The deck was a used Tani-Yakashima, but the trodes were new, still in their shrink wrap. He then gave Jack a code for a rented locker in a Battery Park storage facility, one of several stashes of hard cash he maintained throughout the City. It had more than enough to cover the deck and trodes.

"Thanks," Maddox said. "And keep the change."

"Don't I always?" Jack said with a wink.

The fighter removed his specs, hung them over the neck of his shirt collar. It was a gesture of trust and intimacy, normally followed by words or actions you didn't want recorded in your specs' feed archive. Maddox returned the gesture, removing his own pair.

"So what's going on, amigo?" Jack asked.

"Wish I knew." Maddox removed his bag of tobacco, began to roll a cigarette. "You find out anything?"

Maddox had asked the fighter to make a few discreet calls, see what he could find out. Jack had friends on the police force. He had friends pretty much everywhere. It was one of the advantages of being the smiling, handsome life of the party. Cops were especially fond of him, despite his outlaw status. Natural Jack, the proud warrior who never took fabbed steroids or modded his body to beef up his fight game. A tough bastard who made a living with his fists and smiled while doing it. A man's man who lived by his own code. Cops were suckers for all that macho bullshit.

Jack shook his head. "Not much. None of my friends on the force are working on this one."

Maddox lit a cigarette, felt a stab of disappointment. Without a direct contact on the investigation, whatever Jack might gather from his cop friends would be second- or thirdhand. And cop gossip was like any other gossip, the facts becoming distorted and less reliable with each retelling.

"Any mention of Sanchez?"

"Nothing."

"Nothing?"

"They hadn't even heard of him. Or at least my friends on vice hadn't heard of him."

That struck Maddox as strange. He turned his thoughts back to the botched T-Chen job. He hadn't actually *seen* Sanchez taken into custody in the real world, of course. All he'd witnessed was the man's avatar getting frozen and geotagged, then disappearing. The arrest Maddox had inferred, a conclusion based on similar arrests he'd seen— sometimes closer than he would have liked—a dozen or so times over the years.

Had Sanchez managed to get away, somehow evade capture? He hadn't struck Maddox as terribly clever. Or at least not that clever. But anything was possible. Cops screwed up sometimes. Kicked down the wrong door. Slapped handcuffs around the wrong wrists. Shot the wrong people in the face.

He told himself not to overthink it. Jack had only

made a couple calls. It wasn't exactly a comprehensive inquiry of the entire police force. It was still possible—even probable, now that he rethought it— that Sanchez was sitting in a jail cell now and Jack's contacts on the vice squad simply hadn't heard about it yet.

"They tell you anything about the bombing?"

"They brought in some gang for questioning," Jack said.

Maddox blew smoke. "Gang?"

"Yeah, some biker outfit. Call themselves the Anarchy Boyz."

Maddox's cigarette froze halfway to his lips. "Oh, shit."

"You've heard of them?"

"Kind of."

He'd more than heard of the Anarchy Boyz. He'd committed felonies with them. Near the end of his short stint as a salaryman with Latour-Fisher biotech, he'd crossed paths with the motorbiker delinquents. His first impression had them pegged as nothing special. Teen thugs. Wannabe gangsters. But later, when they'd helped him elude a killer AI, his opinion had changed. They were kids, yes. Pimply-faced and hyperactive. Crude and loud. Their lives were gaming and motorbikes and fart jokes. But at the same time, they were stone-cold pros. Clever thieves and deadly dangerous. As lethal as any mercenary crew he'd ever known.

But terrorist bombers? No, that didn't fit. Not even close.

Until Jack had mentioned the Anarchy Boyz, Maddox had held on to the hope this was all some bad coincidence. That whoever had bombed the T-

Chen building had simply picked the worst possible time to do it: while he was datajacking the company's digital assets. But now, with the young bikers implicated in the bombing, he abandoned that notion. Two coincidences was one too many.

He felt as if he were standing on a frozen lake and the ice had begun to break beneath him. In a handful of hours, his entire world had flipped sideways. What the hell was happening? What kind of nightmare had he been pulled into?

He took a long, contemplative draw on his cigarette. The kid, he thought. Maybe the kid would know something.

"So what's the next move, Blackburn?" Jack asked.

Maddox blew smoke, looked at his friend. "I'm going up to Fabbertown."

5
FABBERTOWN

Visiting the Bronx unarmed wasn't generally advisable, and Maddox wasn't packing. But at least he had a bodyguard. Jack had insisted on coming along with Maddox to Fabbertown. Maddox had tried to dissuade him, insisting it was best the fighter stay out of it. Jack wouldn't hear any of it, though, refusing to let Maddox wander Fabbertown alone.

The two had grown up in the same Harlem hiverise on East 134th, which made them turf brothers, turfies for short. For some—and Maddox included himself among these—the connection had little meaning. The fighter was his friend, not because of their common roots, but simply because Jack was everybody's friend. For the fighter, though, the turf bond was thick as blood, and he wasn't about to let a homeboy walk into one the City's dicier areas without someone watching his back.

After a two-hour ride on a teeming, sweaty subway car, they finally emerged from the station, squinting in the bright afternoon sun. Maddox hadn't been to the Bronx in years, and he'd forgotten how much of a

39

barren dump it was. There were no hiverises. No towering holo ads. And only a sparse scattering of hovers moved about overhead. He was only a handful of miles from Manhattan, but it felt like a different world. Different meaning bad.

A lawless sprawl of crumbling brick homes and dilapidated public housing towers from the previous century, the Bronx was perhaps the world's largest squatter's village. Police entered the borough only on rare occasions, usually when some newly elected politician or police chief wanted to make a "tough on crime" statement, inviting the press along for a raid on a pharma fabber's lab or human smuggling operation. The rest of the time, the Bronx was left alone to its own anarchy and squalor. Not the kind of place you visited unless you absolutely had to, Maddox reflected. Which pretty much summed up why he was here.

"This way," Maddox said, gesturing west. "A couple blocks, if I remember right."

A minute later they found the entrance, a rusted metal archway that read BRONX ZOO. A long X was spray painted through the two words, and underneath, in stylized multicolored script, someone had relabeled the sign FABBERTOWN. Maddox and Jack passed under the archway.

As the name implied, the sprawling grounds of the old zoo, with its empty cages and abandoned holding pens long since overgrown with vines and weeds, was a vast commercial bazaar, specializing in fabbed merchandise of every imaginable, and mostly illegal, variety. You could, of course, find illicitly fabricated narcotics and guns and wares elsewhere in the City. But no place had the scale and diversity of selection you found in Fabbertown.

The grounds were subdivided into informal cobbled-together sections where vendors with similar offerings clustered in groups. Maddox and Jack entered Fabbertown at its southernmost section, an area dedicated to pharmaceuticals. A jumbled mass of tents and tables greeted them. Hundreds of improvised stalls and kiosks filled the treeless expanse. Though it looked more like a refugee camp than a shopping bazaar to Maddox, the place had the familiar buzz of a marketplace. Vendors barked their pitches at passersby, and people milled about with the slow deliberation of shoppers in no particular hurry. There was a faintly chemical smell in the air, the kind of odor Maddox associated with narcofabbers.

Holding his gear satchel tight to his body, he reminded himself this was no Midtown plaza market, where families shopped without worry because rhino cops were stationed every half block. Here it was dog-eat-dog. No cops, no law and order. Getting ripped off by a vendor wasn't the worst that could happen to you here. Not by a long shot. Fabbertown was notorious for sudden outbreaks of violence, so Maddox and Jack knew they had to watch their step. The free, unregulated market. It could be a nasty place at times.

The pair snaked their way through the crowded space, ignoring the desperate waves and pitches hollered in their direction. Fabbers the size of tiny ovens sat atop vendor displays, little holos floating above them. Some were words, making outrageous claims. MIRACLE CANCER CURE! and GROW YOUR HAIR BACK TODAY! Others were simply animations or icons, for the illiterate among the shoppers. A cartoon woman swallowing a pill that made her eyes pop wide open and her hair stand on end. A shirtless man flexing through a series of bodybuilder poses, his swollen pecs and biceps rippling. The lower portion of Maddox's specs cycled through a series of one-time discounts and today-only offers as he passed through a succession of short-range broadcast cones.

"Where can I find hover parts?" Maddox asked an old woman. She stood behind a fabber with a holo that read FOUR-HOUR HARD-ON.

She stared at him blankly. "Fifty," she answered.

Maddox sighed. Jesus, just for directions? He felt a tug at his sleeve. Looking down, he saw a grimy-faced kid peering up at him. "I'll tell you for twenty."

Maddox laughed inwardly. The free market. It was never free, but it was often discounted. The lady tried to shoo the kid away, but it was too late. Maddox had already reached into his pocket and pulled out a twenty. As the kid went for it, Maddox snatched it away. "When we get there," he said.

* * *

The kid led them through a dense thicket of trees that opened up into another clearing, this one much smaller than the one near the entrance, but with a similar cluster of shoppers and merchants. The nearest vendor stand had an oversized fabber, roughly a meter square. The kind of device used to fab spare parts for industrial machinery. Above it, a holo of a hover engine slowly rotated.

This was the place. Maddox paid the kid and he scampered away, disappearing into the foliage, bare feet crunching over fallen leaves.

The shoppers here were mostly hobbyists who

worked on their own hovers. There were tinkerers, who simply enjoyed making little, personal modifications to their vehicle. Adhesive light arrays for a glowing underbelly. Faux leather steering columns. Then there were racers, who were less concerned about looks than performance, searching for aftermarket wares like dogs sniffing out a trail, looking for anything that would increase thrust, improve aerodynamics, or reduce vehicle weight.

Scattered throughout the crowd were security guards, patrolling and brandishing automatic rifles. Hired guns contracted by the vendors to keep an eye on things. A few wore full body armor, but most had only a piece or two. A helmet but no chest plate, or only leg armor only. One of them—a man with no helmet and dark wraparound specs—did a double take in Maddox's direction, then turned and hurried over, striding directly at him. Maddox swallowed and glanced around. He was more or less in the center of the clearing. No place to run or hide.

The guard pointed at him. "Hey, you there."

Maddox backed up a step, bumping into Jack's chest.

Jack looked over, spotted the man approaching them. "Aw, hell," the fighter said, his voice falling in disappointment. "Sorry about this."

"Let's get out of here," Maddox said, already turning to leave.

Jack grabbed his friend's arm, stopping him. "We're fine," he said. "Let me handle this. Won't take a minute."

Maddox anxiously pondered what exactly wouldn't take a minute. Jack wasn't armed, and the guard carried a rifle and a holstered handguns on each hip.

And those were just the visible weapons.

The guard stopped a couple meters away, looking them up and down for a moment. Jack stepped in front of Maddox. Removing his specs, the guard revealed a wide-eyed expression of disbelief.

"Natural Jack Kadrey," the man said, "as I live and breathe." His face glowed with awe, the expression of a kid meeting his favorite pro soccer player. "I seen you fight that Mexican a couple years back."

"Salvador Arguello?" Jack asked.

"That's the one," the guard said, snapping his fingers.

Jack shook his head, smiled. "Arguello was one tough hombre. Took me into some deep water that night."

"You knocked him down five times," the guard said, fawning.

"The problem was he kept getting up," Jack laughed. He rubbed his knuckles. "My hands were sore for a week after that fight."

Maddox let out a breath of relief. The guard handed his specs to him. "Hey, man, can you take a pic of us?"

Jack shrugged an apology at Maddox, then turned to the guard. "Sure," he said brightly, "he'd be happy to." After he'd posed with the man, Maddox heard him ask casually, "Say, you wouldn't happen to know a kid around here named Tommy Park, would you?"

The guard pointed them to the far edge of the clearing, where a kid named Tommy had a stall. Still starstruck by Jack, he offered to show them the way, but the fighter kindly refused, shaking the man's hand. "We'll find it, brother. Thank you so much."

Maddox and Jack left the guard and headed toward

the clearing's edge. "So much for staying under the radar," Maddox muttered.

Jack chuckled. "Sorry about that. Gotta stay on the public's good side, you know. They buy tickets that pay the bills."

Maddox blew smoke, not bothering to state the obvious. Jack loved the attention, lived for it, basked in it. The man had never met a stranger.

"There he is," Maddox said, spotting Tommy behind a folding table littered with small bits of machinery. The kid hadn't changed much since Maddox had seen him last, nearly a year ago. Still the skinny, fidgety teen runt he remembered. Smart eyes that didn't miss anything, the kind of heightened awareness predatory animals and street kids had.

The kid's attention was focused on a ponytailed man standing in front of the table, his arms crossed as he eyed the wares scattered on the tabletop. The timeless pose of a skeptical shopper.

The kid reached for a long cigar-shaped part, lifting it carefully, as if it were some fragile, invaluable work of art. "You see this injector?" he asked the ponytailed man. "Just last month I sold four of these to Abel Martinez."

The man made a disbelieving face. "Rocket Martinez?" he scoffed. "Get the fuck out of here."

Tommy held up one hand. "Swear to God, mister. You ever see him race down at the old fairgrounds?"

"Once or twice," Ponytail said.

"He's a homeboy," Tommy said, adding more bullshit to what was already a fairly large pile. "We're from the same block downtown. He gets all his aftermarkets right here." Tommy waved his hand over the gear atop the table with the reverence of a jeweler showing off his personal treasure of precious stones, as if the pieces were something far more valuable than the salvaged or stolen junk they actually were.

The kid half-turned, gestured to a fabber on the ground behind him. Behind the device's thick glass, a light slowly pulsed. "Everything fabbed here is my own personal design. You won't find them anywhere else. You want your machine to run like Rocket's, you're in the right place."

Maddox and Jack stood a short distance away, watching as the ponytailed man took the injector and examined it, turning it over in his hands, feeling its weight. A few moments later, he reached into his pocket, pulled out some bills, and handed them to the kid. As the man wandered away, Maddox and Jack approached the table.

"Nice sale," Maddox said. "He didn't look like the buying type to me."

As the kid recognized Maddox, his surprised expression quickly reshaped itself into an annoyed frown. "What do you want? I'm busy."

Great, the kid was still pissed at him. "Holding a grudge isn't very professional, you know."

"No grudges here, salaryman," the kid said with a cold smile.

"So how's biz?"

"Better than it was with you," Tommy said. "Can't get fired when you're working for yourself, you know."

No grudges, sure. Maddox dropped his cigarette to the dirt, crushed it under his shoe.

"It was just business," Maddox said. "Nothing personal."

The kid laughed sarcastically. "That sounds about right. Nothing's personal with you, is it?" He flicked his chin at Jack. "So, what, you need a bodyguard now?"

"I'm just a friend," Jack said, suppressing a smile, clearly amused by the kid's grit.

"Didn't think Maddox had any friends," the kid said. "Only customers."

Jack laughed. "Damn, Blackburn, what did you to this boy to make him love you so much?"

Maddox gave the fighter a you-don't-want-to-know look, then turned back to the kid. "Water under the bridge, kid. Get over it already."

The kid glared at Maddox, not saying anything. Around them the marketplace buzzed and churned.

"You really design all this stuff yourself?" Jack asked, trying to break the tension by switching topics. The kid rolled his eyes, then squatted down and opened the fabber. He removed a small battery-powered light from inside, the kind a parent leaves in the room of a child frightened by the dark. It pulsed slowly, mimicking the glow of a fabber's printing nozzle. The light made for a convincing illusion. The kid turned it off, replaced it inside the device, and stood back up.

"Sure, I design it all myself," he said, kicking the side of the dead fabber. "With this piece of shit I found on the side of the road."

The fighter laughed, clapped his hands. "I love it. You had me fooled. Good con." The kid's icy front thawed a bit, the smallest hint of a hustler's smile touching his face. Natural Jack could charm the devil himself.

"You heard from the Anarchy Boyz lately?"

Maddox asked.

The kid's smile vanished. "Why do you want to know?"

"When was the last time you saw them?"

The kid stared at him.

"It's important," Maddox urged. "Your turfies are in some very deep shit."

Tommy licked his lips, looked around warily. "Is this about that bombing downtown?" he asked, keeping his voice low.

Maddox and Jack exchanged looks. Maddox leaned forward. "Yeah, it is."

The kid nodded, his features knotting with worry. "I saw something on the feeds about it this morning. Didn't catch all of it, just heard something about a biker gang. So I tried to call my turfies to see if they knew what was going on, but nobody answered."

"You called them?" A stab of dread jabbed Maddox in the gut. "When?"

"About half an hour ago," the kid said.

Maddox turned to Jack. "We've got to get out of here."

Jack didn't respond, his attention fixed on something in the crowd. On some woman, Maddox assumed. "Jack," he repeated, "you hear what I said? We've got to—"

"We got trouble, Blackburn," Jack said, slowly nodding his head toward whatever held his gaze.

Maddox looked, saw a pair of cops in rhino armor at the opposite edge of the clearing. They held automatic rifles and stood next to a woman's merchant stall, their visors down, faces hidden. The woman was saying something to them, nodding emphatically. Then she pointed in Maddox's direction and mouthed the words *right there*.

Time slowed to a near stop as the cops broke into a run, coming straight at them.

6
OFF THE GRID

Fearing a raid, the Fabbertown crowd dispersed in all directions the same way cockroaches scrambled for cover in a dark room suddenly flooded with light. Jack yanked on Maddox's arm, pulling him away. The fighter was saying something, shouting, but Maddox couldn't hear him over the blood pumping in his ears and the panicked cries of the marketplace.

Maddox and Jack fled into the nearest thicket of trees. From behind them came the tinny amplified voice of one of the cops. "Last warning, citizen!"

There hadn't been a first warning. There was never a first warning. Maddox, like anyone who'd grown up on the City's valley floor, had heard the phrase shouted countless times. Usually followed by gunfire.

Maddox ran faster, dodging trees and ducking under low-hanging branches. Jack trailed close behind. Ahead of them, Maddox spotted Tommy darting through the undergrowth.

"The kid!" Jack shouted. "Follow the kid!"

"What?" Maddox protested. Before he could say anything more a burst of gunfire cracked the air. He flinched, then lowered his head and crouched, trying to become a smaller target.

They ran. The trees grew more densely packed together, slowing them down. Maddox held out his hands to keep branches from scratching his face. They were still chasing after Tommy, and somewhere in his mind Maddox realized why Jack thought that made sense. The kid knew the area, probably knew how to get away.

More shots from behind them. A tree trunk next to Maddox exploded into splinters. He weaved his way through the thickening maze of leaves and branches, expecting to feel a bullet strike him at any moment. Then the thicket abruptly ended and they burst upon a large clearing. It was a section of Fabbertown dedicated entirely to food stalls, also emptied of people after the shooting started. Smoke still rose from a taco stand's grill.

"There!" Jack said, pointing. Tommy cut between a pair of stalls and disappeared into the thick trees beyond.

"No," Maddox said, panting. The trees were slowing them down. He spotted a footpath to the left. It looked narrow and winding enough to give them cover, but clear enough of obstructions that they could move at a flat run. They might be able to put some distance between themselves and the cops, whose bulky rhino armor limited speed and mobility.

Maddox pointed. "Look, there!"

Jack peered over, nodded. "Let's go."

They bolted for the path, scrambling across a wide expanse of flat dirt. Easy targets, Maddox thought uneasily. As they hit the opening of the footpath, shots rang out. Maddox flinched as he sprinted around a wall of shrubbery.

"Go, go, go!" Jack cried.

Maddox didn't need to be told. He ran as fast as he could down the winding pathway, ignoring the heavy weariness spreading in his thighs, the burn in his lungs. The path made so many confusing turns and loops they might have been going in a big circle for all he knew. But they seemed to be putting distance between themselves and their pursuers. The amplified voices from behind were still shouting for them to stop, but the sounds grew more distant.

Abruptly, the path exited into another large clearing. Like the previous one, abandoned merchant stalls stood throughout the open space. Maddox and Jack paused, scanning the perimeter for another path. Maddox searched desperately as he took large, gulping breaths.

"I don't see a way out," Jack said, giving voice to the desperate thought Maddox had at the same moment.

"There isn't one," Maddox panted. "It's a dead end."

Maddox ground his teeth together. He wasn't in his element. If he were in the City, he'd have given the cops the slip easily, the same way he had countless times. Scrambling up a fire escape like a monkey, leaping across the gap of neighboring rooftops, ducking into a hidden subway maintenance corridor. He'd evaded the cops so many times in so many ways since childhood, it had become a kind of game to him. It felt like anything but a game at the moment.

Maddox heard the cops lumbering up the footpath. "Hide," he blurted.

They scrambled about, furiously searching the

merchant stalls for a place to hole up. Jack dove inside a small space between stacks of old car tires, balling himself up as small as he could manage, then pulling a couple tires over the gap to hide from view. Maddox squeezed his way inside the empty cabinet of a food kiosk, wedging himself into a tight nook beside a rusted-out gas canister, clutching his gear satchel to his chest. His feet slipped on warm grease that had dripped down from the still-hot cooking surface a couple centimeters above his head. The heat felt like a hot towel lying across his scalp. He reached out, closed the cabinet door, and blinked in the sudden darkness.

A moment later he heard the cops enter the clearing. "Fan out," one of them said. Perfect, Maddox thought morbidly. He'd hoped they wouldn't pause here, that they'd run straight through, assuming he and Jack had run into the trees beyond the clearing. No such luck.

There were holes oxidized into one wall of his hiding place. They were too small for anyone to see him from outside but large enough for him to have a limited view of what was going on. He saw two cops stalking the edge of the clearing, their visored faces moving back and forth in slow, searching sweeps, rifles held at the ready. Then a pair of armored legs blocked the view, passing less than a meter from his face. Clenching his jaw muscles tight, he didn't move, didn't breathe.

He waited, every muscle in his body tense, expecting the cabinet door to fly open at any moment. He heard crashing noises, things being tumbled over. The cops were going through the stalls, tearing them apart. Nothing here, go check that one, he heard one of them say. Sweat ran into Maddox's eyes. He blinked hard, not daring to wipe it away with his hands and maybe bang his elbow against the metal door, revealing himself. Through the holes he saw the edge of the tire stack where Jack was hiding. A cop walked up next to the stack, stopped. Maddox held his breath as the cop kicked the stack, then started to remove a tire.

Maddox flinched at the sudden scream of a motor. A hover engine, winding up to what sounded like red line revolutions. Loud and close.

"Take it down!" one of the cops cried. In the next moment, a barrage of automatic gunfire buried the sound of the hover engine.

Daylight assaulted him as the door to his hiding place flew open. A silhouetted figure loomed over him. Maddox held his hands up reflexively and gasped, anticipating gunshots. None came. Instead, the figure pulled him out by the arm. Jack.

"Quiet now," he said, his mouth close to Maddox's ear. "Come on."

Squinting against the bright light, Maddox couldn't tell what was happening. The gunfire continued as Jack hustled him across the dirt. A moment later, his eyes adjusted enough to glimpse the rhino cops at the opposite side of the clearing, their rifles trained on a smoking hover falling from the sky like a brick.

As they dashed back onto the footpath from which they'd come, the firing stopped, followed by a crunching thud of metal slamming heavily against the ground.

They ran, listening for sounds of pursuit. There was no gunfire, no shouts for them to stop. The distant amplified voices of the cops grew fainter, then disappeared completely. The cops must have continued after them in the same direction, unaware Maddox and Jack had doubled back. The pair slowed to a jog, more from exhaustion than mutual consent. As he caught his breath, Maddox's thoughts turned to Tommy. Had the kid gotten away?

When they emerged a minute later into the clearing where they'd first seen the kid, Maddox had his answer. Tommy was there, kneeling next to his stand, hurriedly packing wares into a large canvas bag. Except for Maddox and Jack, the kid was alone in the large abandoned clearing.

"Well, I'll be damned," Jack said.

The kid jerked his head up at them. "Are the rhinos on you?" he snapped, heaving the bag over his shoulder.

"No," Maddox said, breathing heavily. "What happened? That hover…" He was still too gassed to get out more than a couple words at a time.

Tommy peered beyond them, his brow furrowed. "They'll be back before long." He tilted his head, gesturing for them to follow. "Come on. I know a way out where they won't see us."

*   *   *

The tunnels beneath the old Bronx Zoo had to be at least a couple centuries old, judging by the brickwork. Maddox recognized the same kind of masonry, small, tightly packed bricks dull blond in color, on some of the City's oldest buildings. The ones marked with special plaques, designating them as historical landmarks. Where someone of significance had died. Where some important treaty was signed. The tight, darkened passageways would have been impossible for Maddox to navigate without his specs amplifying the almost nonexistent ambient light.

The air was cool and humid. The walls glistened with moisture. Maddox and Jack followed Tommy, still catching their breath.

"Why didn't you come down here in the first place?" Maddox asked.

The kid answered without turning around. "I couldn't. The cops were blocking the only entrance. I had to circle back around."

"Who was in that hover?" Jack asked.

"No idea," the kid said. "But those rhinos weren't messing around."

No, they hadn't been, Maddox agreed inwardly. They hadn't even bothered to warn the hover's driver, which their rhino gear could do by overriding the vehicle's audio system. Instead, they'd opened fire without hesitating. Not exactly standard procedure.

Maddox swallowed. Those cops hadn't been looking to arrest someone. They were a hit squad.

For the next few minutes, no one spoke. Condensation dripped from the ancient arched ceiling. Their footfalls echoed softly off the walls. Maddox finally felt his heart return to something close to a normal rhythm.

Slowly, the darkness dissipated. The dank, heavy atmosphere gave way to a cool current of air. They were nearing an exit.

"So where does this come out?" Jack asked.

"About a block from a metro station," Tommy said.

A minute later, they climbed a narrow stairway and emerged into the sunlight. Tommy pressed his hand against his forehead to block the sudden brightness. The Bronx spread out quietly around them. Empty lots overgrown with weeds, decaying buildings, cracked and crumbling roadways that looked as if they'd been beaten by an angry god wielding an enormous hammer. Roughly fifty meters in front of them stood an elevated metro platform. A small knot of people milled about at the top of the stairs, waiting for the next train.

Standing there, it occurred to Maddox he hadn't given any thought to his next move. Beyond getting back to the City, that was. If he had any chance of staying one step ahead of the cops, it was in the crowded sprawl of the City's valley floor, where he knew dozens of ways to stay off their radar. Yes, the cops had caught him off guard when they'd raided his office, and yes, he still didn't know how they'd managed to locate his place of business. But even so, he felt the odds had evened up a bit. Certainly not in his favor, but at least now he knew they were after him. Now they couldn't surprise him. What he needed was a place to hole up, catch his breath, and see if he could figure out what the hell was going on.

"So what's our next stop?" Jack asked.

"*Our* next stop?" Maddox said. "This is where you get off the roller coaster, Jack. I'm toxic, in case you haven't noticed."

Jack waved a hand dismissively. "A little heat. Big deal."

"This is more than a little heat," Maddox said.

Jack nodded, as if that was just what he wanted to hear. "All the better. I could use a new story to add to my legend," he said shamelessly, then glanced at Tommy and gave the kid a playful wink. "And besides, everybody knows Jack Kadrey doesn't cut and run."

The kid's eyes widened. "Wait, you're Jack Kadrey? Natural Jack Kadrey, the fighter? Holeeey shit!" His anger at Maddox instantly forgotten, the kid gawked upward, his mouth hanging open. The fighter smiled, basking in the kid's awed stare.

"At your service, little brother," he said with a gracious nod.

Maddox resisted the urge to roll his eyes. "Okay, big shot, listen to me. I didn't see any bee drones back there, so you're probably not burned. But if you stick around this party much longer, you will be. So right about now, cutting and running would be the smartest thing you could do." After a moment he added: "In fact, doing anything *besides* cutting and running would be monumentally stupid."

Jack smiled at the kid. "It's like he's daring me to stick around, isn't he, young brother?"

The kid was still gawking. "You are *such* a badass," he mooned.

This time Maddox didn't resist the urge and rolled his eyes. He smoked, taking a long drag and blowing out. The fighter stared at him, grinning in a way that told Maddox he had no chance of talking Jack out of it. The man's turf loyalty ran deep.

There was a low rumble in the distance, growing louder. A metro train approaching. "Your call," he told the fighter, shrugging. So Jack wanted to play the superhero. Fine. Maddox was too tired to argue the point.

The trio headed to the metro station, climbed the stairs. As they stepped up onto the platform, Maddox scanned the area for security cams. There was a single rusted-out housing high on the wall, a pair of bare wires snaking out from it that had once been attached to a camera. They moved to an empty space, away from the half dozen people waiting for the train.

"I know a safe place off the grid," Jack suggested, keeping his voice low, "where we can lay low for a spell."

"Sounds good," Tommy said.

It sounded anything but good to Maddox. Splitting up was their best option. Together, they were conspicuous as hell. A huge black guy, an average white guy, and a Korean kid. Even if the cops hadn't managed to get a clear pic of them back in Fabbertown, by now they'd surely put together a description. And it would take all of ten seconds to send out a search algorithm to every street cam and bumblebee drone in the City, tweaked to find just such a trio.

Still, he needed to find out what Tommy knew about this whole mess, if indeed he knew anything. The cops had interrupted him before he could ask the kid much of anything. A couple hours of downtime with some space to breathe might get a few of his questions answered. Then after that, they'd have to split up.

The train roared its arrival to the station. The clackety-clack of the tracks slowed and brakes shrieked as the train reduced speed and the graffiti-covered cars shuddered to a stop.

"All right," Maddox told Jack as the doors slid open. "So where are we going?"

"I know the perfect place," Jack said, his tone a bit more enthusiastic than the occasion called for.

"And you're sure it's off the grid?" Maddox asked.

"Utterly and totally. Trust me."

7
ELECTRIC KITTY

Jack brought them to a brothel, of course. It was a very Jack way of going underground.

"Who said going off the grid can't be fun?" Jack said, elbowing Maddox playfully as they stepped into the run-down tenement in Queens. They were greeted warmly by the hostess, a fiftyish woman named Celeste with intricate face tattoos and forearms full of jangling silver bracelets. She hugged Jack around the neck and fussed over him and his companions like an overbearing mother. Sex workers in various states of undress brought them generous portions of stir-fried noodles and glasses of cold beer. Tommy hardly spoke as he slurped his noodles, his wide eyes wandering from woman to woman. More than once Maddox noticed the distracted kid miss his mouth with his chopsticks, poking a load of greasy noodles against his cheek.

Electric Kitty—a place Maddox had heard of once or twice but had never visited before today—catered to body mod fetishists, employing sex workers with an impressive variety of surgical and nano-enabled modifications. Pigtailed anime girls in plaid skirts with flawless pink skin and enlarged irises and pupils. Living, breathing porn cartoons, giggling and sucking on lollipops. A topless woman with bright blue skin, devil horns, and yellow cat's eyes. A toffee-skinned geisha with full lips and dreadlocked hair who looked to Maddox as if (s)he occupied the exact midpoint of the gender spectrum. A man with rippling muscles and a deep tan, his right arm below the elbow missing, replaced with a sex machine prosthetic. Dildo fingers of varying shapes and sizes. By the time Maddox finally noticed the woman with two rows of tits, he'd already lost the ability to be surprised.

Maddox was less than comfortable with Jack's selected refuge, but he had to admit the fighter had been right about the place. Electric Kitty was indeed off the grid. The scramble shields embedded in the walls and ceilings that housed the four-story operation were top of the line, blocking all incoming and outgoing digital traffic. As soon as they'd arrived, Maddox kicked off an app in his specs, checking for vulnerabilities and security gaps. The app had run through its routines and, to Maddox's great relief, found nothing. The place was watertight. A tiny island of digital darkness in a cybernetic sea. Even the ad feed went silent in Maddox's lenses, which almost never happened. A large portion of the operation's clientele, apparently, wanted their secret desires to stay that way, so Electric Kitty, ever attentive to its customers' wishes, invested heavily in privacy tech, making it an ideal place for the trio to hide.

After the meal, Celeste showed them to a spacious ground-floor room near the rear of the building. The fighter sat on an overstuffed burgundy sofa, a woman on either side of him, a third sitting on his lap. Tommy sat awkwardly in a chair that matched the sofa. Maddox wondered if the kid's uncomfortable expression was worry for his friends, or if it was simply the sex-anxiety of a first brothel visit. A bit of both, maybe.

Maddox looked at Jack, shook his head.

"What?" Jack asked, his voice rising with exaggerated innocence, his large hands full of ass. "You wanted to go off the grid, so I got you off the grid."

Getting off the grid. Getting off, period. Why not do both at the same time? Yes, Maddox thought again, this was a very Jack way of going underground.

*   *   *

Convincing Jack to downshift his revving sex engine wasn't easy, but Maddox persisted. Finally the fighter gave in, at least for the moment, and politely asked the women to give them some privacy. Alone and nakedfaced, the three huddled around a small table with Maddox's gear satchel lying on top of it.

"All right, kid," Maddox began, "give it up. What's going on with your turfies?"

"I told you already," the kid insisted. "I don't know anything. I tried to call them and I didn't get through to anybody." Tommy stared hard at Maddox. "But what if they did blow up some office? Why would you give two shits, salaryman?"

Salaryman. Before today, Maddox hadn't been called that in a while. Not since he and Tommy and a mercenary woman named Beatrice had gotten mixed up with a very nasty AI. Beatrice had called him salaryman, her voice inflected with either sarcasm or contempt—he'd never been sure which it was. Here with Tommy, it was a hundred percent, unmistakable contempt. The kid was still carrying a grudge.

After their run-in with the AI, Maddox had taken Tommy under his wing, not unlike his late mentor Rooney had done with him once upon a time. The kid had the innate skill needed for datajacking, and in the early days of rebuilding his business, Maddox had needed the help. Tommy had been a quick study, taking only weeks to learn the ins and outs of core-level virtual space. For most newbies it took months.

But the kid had proved to be too undisciplined, too inclined to ignore Maddox's guidance. The overeager kid would jump headlong into something right after he'd been instructed to move cautiously. Tommy was ambitious and impatient to the point of recklessness, and Maddox couldn't afford to employ a bull in his china shop. After a couple frustrating months, he'd cut the kid loose.

In the year since, Maddox had slowly, painstakingly rebuilt his business. And in the last few months, the work had finally found a decent rhythm. Jobs were coming in steadily, cash flow was growing. Then this mess had hit him, knocking him down just when he'd gotten back on his feet, for reasons he couldn't fathom. Maddox had never been a starry-eyed optimist. When things were going well, the larger part of him never expected it to last. The good times were the exception to the rule, the smallest sections on the timeline of your life. But even a cynic to the marrow might have expected a run of good luck to last more than a few short months. And it was this that angered him most about his sudden and mysterious reversal of fortune. He'd worked himself to the bone, scratched and clawed his way to the threshold of success, peered into its room, only to have the door slammed shut in his face.

Some of the anger in Tommy's face faded, then a light flipped on behind his eyes, like he'd finally figured out some nagging problem. "I just got it," the kid said.

"Got what?" Maddox asked.

"The cops think *you* have something to do with that bombing, too, don't they?"

Maddox didn't answer. The kid might be reckless, but he wasn't stupid. He hadn't planned on looping the kid in, but so much for that.

"Should have known," the kid said, shaking his head. "You don't care they're in jail. You only care because it touches you."

"I'm sorry for wanting to stay out of jail."

"And what about my turfies?" the kid said.

"What about them?"

"They saved your ass, if you remember. You owe them, salaryman."

"Stop calling me salaryman," Maddox said. "And your turfies saved *your* ass, not mine."

It was true and it wasn't. The biker gang *had* come to Tommy's rescue while the kid was running interference for Maddox during a datajacking run. But it was also true that if they hadn't shown up when they did, Maddox might not have been able to pull off his part of the job.

He took a long draw on his cigarette. The tip glowed to life as he inhaled, tobacco sizzling. "Listen, kid," he said, blowing, "there's nothing I can do to help them."

"Like you would if you could," the kid muttered.

Maddox ignored the comment. "I don't even

know what this is all about. I'm trying to find out."

The kid sat there for a moment. "So the cops think you're a terrorist now, huh?"

Maddox blew out a tired breath. "I don't know what they think."

"*Are* you a terrorist?" the kid asked pointedly.

"Not this week," Maddox answered glibly, then turned the question around. "But what about your turfies? Did they go and get themselves radicalized? They get off on bombing business offices now? Sticking it to the corporate man?"

The kid looked offended. "That's not how they roll. They don't care about City Hall and bullshit politics."

Maddox said, "This is the part where I remind you they call themselves the Anarchy Boyz."

"So what?" the kid said.

"The name implies a certain political leaning, yeah?" Maddox blew smoke.

The kid rolled his eyes. "It's just a badass name, that's it. Bombing a building? They don't pull stuff like that."

Maddox took a long drag. He tended to believe the kid. Despite their name, the Anarchy Boyz had never struck him as having any kind of activist agenda or social axe to grind. They were delinquents, thieves, scam artists, certainly, but they weren't terrorists.

He blew out a disappointed cloud of smoke. The kid was a bust. He didn't know anything helpful, wasn't holding any pieces to the puzzle. Maddox was as much in the dark now as he'd been before they'd made the trek up to the Bronx.

"Let me call my friends down on vice squad again," Jack suggested, seeming to sense Maddox's frustration.

Maddox frowned. He'd been mulling over that very action for the last few minutes. "I don't think so."

Jack straightened up. "Why not?"

He tapped his cigarette over an ashtray next to his gear satchel. "You start asking around too much, and they'll wonder why you're so curious."

Jack waved a dismissive hand. "Give me a little credit, Blackburn. You think I don't know how to talk around something? All I have to say is I'm looking for some extra security for my next fight. Hell, there ain't a cop down there who doesn't have some kind of side hustle, legal or otherwise. Then I make a bit of small talk. How's the family? How are things going on the job? You'd be surprised how much a cop will give up about what's going on down at the precinct." He made a talking puppet with his hand. "Chatty as hell, most cops I know."

"Look," Maddox said, "like I said before, I don't think they IDed you up in the Bronx. You need to walk away now. This is a lot of heat." Jack might have been the king of the underground fighting circuit, but he wasn't a career criminal. And this strange mess Maddox found himself in was the kind of deep water he knew the fighter couldn't comprehend, much less navigate. Natural Jack Kadrey could charm his way out of a lot of situations, but this wasn't one of them.

Jack stared at Maddox for a long moment, then turned to the kid. "My friend Blackburn here ever tell you about Rooney?"

Tommy blinked and shook his head.

"Old Rooney took our man Blackburn here off the street, taught him his trade. And back when I was getting started in the fight game, Rooney hooked me up with some promoters, helped me get the ball rolling."

"Jack," Maddox blurted out, "The old man doesn't have anything to do with—"

"You think this Rooney could help us now?" the kid asked Jack.

"He passed on a while back, young brother," Jack said. "But if he were still here, he'd give us a hand. You could count on that."

Jack paused for a moment, then went on. "Yeah, they don't make them like Rooney anymore." The fighter's voice took on a solemn tone, and a wistful expression came over his face. "It's dog-eat-dog here in the City. Everybody's got an angle. Maybe it's always been like that, not just here but everywhere else too. Maybe that's just people, you know?" He glanced over at Maddox. "But when Rooney was around, it reminded you things didn't have to be that way. Not all the time, anyway."

Maddox didn't say anything. He took a long drag on his cigarette. "Fine, but don't say I didn't warn you."

The fighter smiled. "Duly noted, my brother." He then held up a finger. "One call. That's all I'm going to make. And I promise I'll be careful. And who knows?" Jack shrugged. "Maybe I'll get lucky this time. Like I said, cops are chatty, and maybe Gideon's investigation—"

Whatever the end of the sentence was, Maddox didn't hear it. "Gideon," he blurted, interrupting the fighter. "You said Gideon."

"Yeah," Jack said. "Naz Gideon. He's running the bombing investigation."

"You didn't say that before," Maddox pointed out.

"Sure I did," the fighter said.

"No, you didn't," Maddox said. "I would have remembered."

Jack straightened up. "So you know him or something?"

Maddox barely heard the question. The name set off a hundred whirling thoughts in his mind.

He gazed earnestly into the fighter's face. "Forget the call for now. I need to check something first." He removed the deck and trode set from his satchel.

Tommy looked at the equipment, confused. "You're going to plug in?" the kid asked. "Thought you said it was too risky."

Maddox crushed out his cigarette in the ashtray. "Yeah, it is."

8
A DETECTIVE'S REMORSE

The smell of the small room turned Detective Deke's stomach. It was the kind of stink that hung in the air, thick and pervasive, and attached itself to you like humidity in the tropics. A stink that made you deliberately close your mouth to keep out any of its vile airborne molecules. Deke swallowed hard to keep from gagging as a fresh wave hit him. The shit-and-piss stench he could handle. It was the regular rounds of vomiting that got to him. The three odors combined was something from hell, and it nearly made him empty his stomach the same way the four suspects had been emptying theirs for the last hour. The smell of torture and human suffering. Christ, it was nasty.

A couple meters in front of him, a pair of off-duty beat cops in puke-splattered plastic smocks took turns prodding four biker punks with shocksticks. The teenage punks, suspects in the T-Chen Engineering bombing, sat in metal folding chairs, their lanky frames strapped to the chair back and legs, their arms behind them and bound at the wrists. Each punk was a reeking, soaking mess, pants soaked from waist to knees with the foul mixture of their own fluids. Around the third or fourth shock, they'd each lost control of their bowels and bladders.

The taller of the two cops poked the working end of his shockstick into the side of the leftmost youth. The punk's body went rigid, his face contorting grotesquely from the voltage, a guttural, animal sound erupting from his mouth. Deke winced and looked away.

Next to the detective stood Lieutenant Gideon, his commanding officer, who watched the session impatiently, apparently unbothered by the stench. There was a tightness in Gideon's square jaw and a manic quality behind his dark eyes, telltales Deke had learned to spot over the two years they'd worked together. His superior was losing his patience—not that he had much to lose in the first place—and Deke sensed the man was close to boiling over.

In his early thirties, Gideon was younger than Deke by some ten years, but what his boss on the police force lacked in age, he more than made up for in ambition. And in Deke's twenty years as a cop, he'd found that ambition and an irritable impatience often went hand in hand.

Deke self-consciously touched his specs again, which were hanging on his shirt collar, making sure they were turned off. Like Lieutenant Gideon and the two cops dealing out the torture, Deke was nakedfaced. There would be no visual record of what would be officially logged as a voluntary interrogation. And no sound of the session would travel beyond the room, thanks to the thick layer of soundproof foam covering every inch of the ceiling and walls.

The punks didn't know anything useful. That much was obvious to Deke. They barely seemed to know this datajacker Maddox, much less where he was. The punks had reached their breaking point half an hour ago, though the tough one—the girl, of course—had held out a respectable fifteen minutes longer. After twenty years on the force, you got a sense for these things, and Deke had become something of an expert in spotting the exact moment someone's spirit was broken.

It hadn't been a good day for his boss. The one hot lead they'd had, the kid Tommy Park, who'd called each of the punks' specs from a market up in the Bronx, had turned out to be a bust. The kid had managed to slip away from the rhino squad Gideon dispatched to pick him up. The lieutenant had been furious over the squad's failure, and Deke knew his boss would make sure every one of them paid for the screw-up. A month on foot patrol in a hiverise without body armor. Or maybe a few weeks of ground traffic duty at the Five Points. Talk about your hell on earth. The soles of his feet ached just thinking about it.

Still, given the opportunity, Deke would have traded places with any of them in a heartbeat. They weren't nearly in as much hot water as he was. Or maybe the better analogy was a vat of acid, because that was what it felt like he'd been thrown into. Like the floor had suddenly opened under his feet and he'd fallen down into something that would destroy him.

This whole thing had gone too far. He'd been foolish to agree to it in the first place. Why had he let himself get talked into it? Why hadn't he pushed back more?

Still, the situation hadn't yet spiraled completely out of control. And while they couldn't change the regrettable damage that had already been done, they could still get out of this mess if they were careful. They could still dodge the bullet coming their way.

The only problem was convincing Gideon. The lieutenant, it seemed, believed he was bulletproof.

Deke cleared his throat and spoke in a low, confidential tone. "Maybe we should wrap it up," he suggested, worried about more complications if they stretched out the interrogation much longer. The beauty of the shockstick was that, when wielded by experienced hands, it left no marks on the skin or detectable nerve damage, making it the perfect torture device. Its biggest downside was the cumulative risk that came with overuse. The more shocks the punks received, the more likely something bad might happen. Deke had seen suspects stroke out or go into cardiac arrest after only half a dozen shocks, and these punks had already received twice that many. It was one thing to doctor a log entry, tagging the session as a routine interrogation where (whoops!) the feed on your specs also coincidentally failed. It was something else entirely to have to cover up an accidental death. The last thing Deke and the lieutenant needed right now was a second fatal mishap.

Gideon didn't seem to share this concern. He shot Deke an annoyed glance and didn't answer.

The detective swallowed. "If they knew anything useful," he said, "they would have given it up by now."

Gideon snorted. "That your expert opinion? Or

you just pussying out as usual?"

"I'm not pussying—"

"Bullshit," Gideon interrupted. "For the past half hour, you've been standing there, looking like some virgin chick staring a foot-long cock."

"I don't like the direction this is going," Deke said.

"Then maybe you should leave the room."

"I'm talking about all of it," Deke said, keeping his voice low. "Not just these punks."

The lieutenant's expression darkened. His stare was like a heat laser boring into Deke's skull.

"I'm just saying we should slow down and rethink all of this," Deke said. He glanced warily over at the beat cops, lowering his voice further. "It wasn't supposed to go down like this."

Scowling, Gideon regarded his subordinate skeptically, his glare unwavering as one of the biker punks screamed in agony.

After a moment's contemplation, the lieutenant said, "Let's have a chat in my office."

Gideon opened the door. "Back in a minute," he told the beat cops. The pair looked at him with uncertain expressions.

"What are you staring at?" Gideon snapped. "I didn't say stop, did I? Hit them again."

*   *   *

Lieutenant Naz Gideon's office was a four-walled tribute to its occupant. Plaques with his name bestowing various honors and recognitions. Service medals behind glass frames. A picture of him shaking hands with the mayor. This was the office of someone on the fast track, the decor announced to all who entered. Of one of the department's brightest shining stars. Deke never failed to marvel at the excessive shamelessness, at the naked ambition it not so tactfully communicated. But that was Gideon, wasn't it? The runaway locomotive. The raging bull. Step in his way at your own risk.

Gideon sat behind his desk, hands folded, seemingly relaxed. "Have a seat," he said. The anger from minutes earlier appeared to be gone, Deke noted. Maybe that was a good sign.

Deke remained standing, too restless from worry to sit. He paced back and forth in front of the desk. Would the man listen to reason? Would he see just how crazy this whole thing had become?

"This has all gone too far," said the detective.

The lieutenant smiled patiently. "You worry too much, Mr. Sanchez."

"That's not funny," Deke blurted. "I never would have agreed to go undercover with that datajacker if I'd known..." He couldn't bring himself to say it.

Gideon sighed. "Deke, sit down. Please."

After a moment's hesitation, Deke lowered himself onto the chair.

"Can I get you something?" the lieutenant offered as he pulled a small bottle and two glasses from a drawer. "Whiskey?"

"I'm fine."

Gideon poured one for himself, picked up the glass, swirled the amber liquid around. "You need to calm down. This will all be over soon enough." He drank. "You've got nothing to worry about."

"Nothing to worry about?" Deke tapped himself on the chest. "I'm the one who was plugged in with Maddox. What if I get made?"

"You won't. The bogus profile you were using was untraceable, and the forged background was watertight. Maddox didn't suspect you were anyone but who you said you were, did he? And it's all gone now anyway. I made sure of that." He slid his palms together like he was washing his hands. "Mr. Sanchez never existed. I purged it all myself."

Deke took a long breath, though it failed to calm him. True, he had to admit, the cover ID and its manufactured history had worked as planned. A datajacker of Maddox's purported talents wouldn't have been easy to fool, but Gideon had managed to do just that. The lieutenant had even predicted how the jacker would sabotage the fictitious Mr. Sanchez's cloaking app. Still, not everything had gone as planned.

"People died," Deke said bluntly.

Gideon's glass stopped halfway to his mouth. He placed it on the desk, stared at Deke for a long moment. "Regrettable," he said.

Regrettable, yes, Deke agreed cynically. This whole wicked business was regrettable. Gideon's obsession with this datajacker was regrettable. The plan to frame him was regrettable. Deke's stupid, stupid decision to go along with it—hoping to curry favor with the department's brightest star and revive his flailing career—was regrettable.

And most regrettable of all was the bomb's mistimed detonation, which had taken the lives of fourteen T-Chen Engineering employees. The device, smuggled in by a hijacked janitor bot and hidden in a cleaning supplies closet, was supposed to go off at two in the morning, when the building was empty except for a few security bots roaming the hallways. They weren't sure what had happened, why it had blown up during business hours. Someone might have found it and accidentally set it off. Or maybe the timer had failed. For Deke, the question of how it had occurred no longer mattered. As soon as the news of the bombing hit the news feeds and the body count had begun, he'd felt as if the walls were closing in on him. He was an accomplice to murder. Mass murder. And Gideon expected him not only to go about his business as if nothing had happened, which was insane enough, but the lieutenant also refused to abandon his plan to nail this Maddox person to the wall. In Deke's view, it was a course of action that wasn't merely flirting with disaster, it was brazenly inviting it to ruin your life.

"Naz, we have to stop this before it goes any further," Deke pleaded.

"It's too late for that now." Gideon took another drink. "We're too far down the road to turn back."

Deke wasn't so sure about that, retracing the chain of events that were supposed to happen if everything had gone to plan.

Since the datajacker was too slippery, too clever to be caught by conventional police methods, the idea had always been to collar the biker kids first— Maddox's last known associates—and then coerce them into a confession over the T-Chen bombing. Their guilt in the crime was plausible, given not only their criminal histories and lack of credible alibis but also the fact that one of their number, a kid named Tommy Park, ran a junk stand in Fabbertown that sold tech of all sorts, including the kind that one might use to build an explosive device. Tommy Park and the Anarchy Boyz had turned out to be the ideal patsies.

Not so coincidentally, on the same day of the

bombing, there would be a major security breach inside T-Chen's datasphere. As the investigation moved forward, Gideon would make sure the digital and physical crimes were inextricably linked and that Maddox was identified as the mastermind behind both the bomb attack and the DS breach. Only a radicalized extremist would commit such an attack, a cold-blooded terrorist intent on fomenting chaos and misery.

If you wanted to destroy a person, setting them up on a terrorism charge was about the best way to do it. And as soon as one of the Anarchy Boyz broke and confessed, things would start churning in that direction. Gideon would make sure all the dots connected, building a watertight investigation that led inexorably to the datajacker Blackburn Maddox.

For the moment things had stalled, thanks to the Anarchy Boyz's ability to hold out under torture. But Gideon was undeterred and patient, knowing he held all the cards, knowing the confession would come in time. He had to ensure the preplanned fake investigation behaved the same way a real one did, moving forward in logical stages, expanding into new branches of inquiry as new information was discovered. Once the punks confessed, he'd then search for any known contacts with data security expertise. After filtering down to a short list of names, he'd zero in on Maddox, the only one capable of penetrating the state-of-the-art security inside T-Chen's datasphere. The last piece of the puzzle, the icing on the cake, would be when one of the Anarchy Boyz flipped (and one of them inevitably would), cutting a deal for reduced jail time in exchange for naming Maddox as the ringleader.

It hadn't been a bad plan. Genius in its own devious way, Deke had thought at one time. But now, with fourteen dead, he felt entirely different about it. The whole thing was a huge mistake, a monumental lapse of judgment unlike any he'd ever made before. He couldn't see it any other way. It was time to abort, to walk away from the scene of the bloody accident they'd caused. To run away from it, in fact.

"We chase down false leads all the time," Deke pointed out. "We question people for hours over a hit-and-run, only to find out later there was street cam footage of them thirty blocks away. If we let those kids go now, who would question it? Just another bad lead that went nowhere. Then we can put this whole thing behind us."

Bombings, even headline-grabbing ones with massive fatalities, went unsolved more often than not in the City. Gideon knew that as well as Deke did. Like they both also knew that if they cut those punks loose now, before they confessed, they could be done with the whole stinking business. They could chase their tails for a few weeks, running down empty leads until the press coverage died down, then file the case away with the rest of the City's unsolved ugliness.

"I can't do that," Gideon said.

"Can't or won't?" Deke asked.

The lieutenant finished his drink, placed the glass down firmly. He spoke in an even, measured tone, staring at Deke without blinking. "Here's what you're going to do. You're going to take a pill or smoke a joint or do whatever you need to do to get yourself through this thing, you understand? We're not stopping now."

Beneath the lieutenant's quiet resolve and icy stare,

Deke sensed a barely contained explosion, a volcano ready to erupt. He flinched as the lieutenant rose from his chair, then came around and stood in front of him. Gideon placed his hands on Deke's chair arms and leaned down, his face uncomfortably close to the detective's.

"You'll do what I tell you to do. Nothing more, and nothing less. You got me?"

Deke smelled the whiskey on the lieutenant's breath. He turned his head, looked away.

"There's no walking away from this," the lieutenant added. "And there's no walking away from me."

Deke felt his resolve wilting under the weight of Gideon's gaze. A knock on the door broke the tension, and the detective was immediately thankful for the interruption.

Gideon released his grip on the chair and straightened his back. "What is it?" he barked at the door, which opened to reveal Flagler, a pale, pimply-faced security analyst who'd just completed his second year on the job. Flagler was one of Gideon's plants in the data security department.

The analyst removed his specs and took a tentative step into the room. He looked anxiously between Deke and the lieutenant, seemingly aware he'd intruded on some heavy conversation.

"You've got something for me?" Gideon said impatiently.

"We've got a breach," the analyst said. "Someone just pinged your personnel history, and it doesn't look authorized."

A wry smile touched Gideon's mouth. "Does he know you saw him?" he asked, quickly sliding open a large desk drawer. The lieutenant was suddenly animated, energized by the analyst's news.

"I don't think so," Flagler answered. "He's still in there."

"Somebody's pulling your personnel history?" Deke said, curious but mostly alarmed.

Gideon waved him quiet and asked the analyst, "You didn't log it, did you?"

"No, sir. You told me to contact you first if somebody pinged your file."

"Good boy," the lieutenant said, nodding. "Do me a favor and keep it quiet. I'm going to take care of it."

Gideon removed his custom Hasegawa deck and a set of trodes from a drawer and placed them on top of the desk. "Anyone else know?" he asked.

Flagler shook his head. "No, sir. I put the auto alerts on standby and routed all unusual traffic to my desk, just like you asked."

"Perfect," he said, a hunter's thrill in his eyes as he powered up the deck.

9
HELLO, OLD FRIEND

Breaking into the Greater New York City Police Department's datasphere wasn't generally a good idea. It was, in fact, an excellent way to get yourself put away for life, should you be caught in the act. It wasn't like carving out and reselling a bit of proprietary R&D from some consulting company out of Lithuania nobody ever heard of. That would only get you tossed in the can for five to ten, maybe a tad less if you had a good lawyer or you lucked out and got a judge who took donations under the table. Datajacking Johnny Law was another level of criminality altogether, punishable by the same kind of sentences they slapped on serial killers and narco kingpins.

When he'd fired up his deck minutes earlier, Maddox had considered such dire consequences for exactly three seconds before shrugging them off. At some point you were in so much trouble that a bit more didn't make a difference. The needle on his how-screwed-you-are gauge had already moved well into the red zone.

After plugging in, Maddox hit a black market app vendor where he still had a credit balance and loaded up on apps. Then he went to check out his newly formed suspicions about Sanchez, the turncoat corporati who'd hired him to break into T-Chen's datasphere. It took about a half an hour to piece together that the man had never existed, that his identity and background were manufactured. Maddox kicked himself for not checking thoroughly enough the first time around, for failing to crosscheck Social Security records and educational history and captures from cam feeds. It was tedious work and Maddox had been lazy, verifying the man's identity by only the most superficial—and in hindsight, easily spoofed— digital records available to him. He could almost hear Rooney chiding him about being sloppy. Sloppy gets you arrested. Sloppy gets you killed. You have to do your homework. Rikers Island is filled with data thieves who took shortcuts.

The mystery of Sanchez's identity solved—or partially solved, anyway—Maddox now hovered in virtual space, readying himself for his second, far more difficult, task. A short distance away, the pulsing glow of the police department's DS dominated his field of vision, a luminous city of geometric data structures. He breathed, feeling a deep rush of air fill his lungs back in the room at the Electric Kitty as he let himself slide into a trancelike concentration. Every breath took him farther away from the awareness of his body, from his sack of meat and bones and blood, from the limits of the physical. He floated motionlessly, an invisible ghost in the digital ether, occupying the last grid vector of free space beyond the department's security boundary. A thief peering through a barbed-wire fence.

Cops didn't like strangers poking around in their data. Understandable, of course, when you considered how much they had to hide. Bribes, evidence tampering, setups, cover-ups, forged warrants, tortured confessions, abuses of power from the lowliest beat cop's weekly payoff all the way up to the chief of police's insider trading. It was all there, if you looked hard enough. Buried inside interdepartmental communications or archived spec feeds or surveillance footage. Cops were better than most at covering their tracks, but in the end they were people. And people always slipped up. It was human nature. And in a world where every millisecond of your life existed in two states, physical and digital, it was the rare human folly that wasn't captured and filed away in an archive somewhere. Secret sins were things of a bygone era, like tube television sets and gas-powered cars. The cybernetic gods were omnipresent and omniscient. They recorded everything and forgot nothing.

He dispatched half a dozen looksee bots around the datasphere. Like him, they were hidden from detection by a cloaking algorithm. As long as he and the bots remained cloaked and outside the security perimeter, it was unlikely they'd be seen by the DS's automated scans. Once inside, though, things would be different. Cloaks, even the best ones, eventually broke down under the passive countermeasures usually found inside a DS, melting away like an ice cube on a hot sidewalk. The shitty thing about it was you never knew quite how long you had before the cloak disappeared entirely. It depended on how resistant your cloak's algorithm was to begin with, but it also depended on the robustness of the DS's security. A large, dense block of ice survived longer under the tepid heat of a November sun than it did in the scorching heat of July, using the same analogy. How much attention you attracted to yourself also came into play. If you rushed in, knocking holes through archive barriers, not taking care to cover your tracks and clumsily calling attention to yourself, odds were you'd get noticed. Intelligent sentries roamed the DS on the lookout for digital anomalies, and they were adept at detecting the bull-in-a-china-shop types, even when those bulls were fully cloaked.

Datajacking was like any other kind of thievery in that it favored practitioners who took a careful, deliberate, cool-headed approach. The smash-and-grab cowboys who didn't do their homework, who burst headlong into a DS without studying its structure, never lasted very long.

The bots' feeds appeared, six small text boxes winking to life in front of him. Data scrolled upward: authentication parameters of the department's razorwalls, build versions of its intelligent sentries, the manufacturing specs of its passive countermeasures. A mother lode of intelligence gathered by digital spies. The data was cross-referenced with known design flaws, summarizing them for Maddox in a separate window, while predictive models offered up a list of potential vulnerabilities. Green for very likely, yellow for probable, red for you probably shouldn't try this unless you want to go to jail. The bots also gave him a detailed map of the entire DS, complete with labels pairing each of the myriad structures with their real-world analogs. Human resources, payroll, public relations, and so on.

Maddox studied the details, absorbing the information as much by intuition as conscious scrutiny. Eventually a kind of map formed in his mind. The safest path through the minefield. A route that was still dangerous, still risky, and by no means a sure thing, but one that at least lessened his chance of detection. Lessened, but far from eliminated, he thought grimly. Under normal circumstances, he'd take hours, even days, studying a DS's infrastructure, obsessively poring over every security app's soft spots and setting up sandbox environments to test different intrusion approaches. But here and now, he didn't have the luxury of time.

Back in the room, his hands gestured, and in virtual space he moved slowly forward, past the unseen line marking the edge of the department's outermost security boundary. Here at the periphery, he didn't worry too much about being detected. His cloaking app was state-of-the-art, more than a match for the department's relatively weak first line of defense, which was something akin to an unguarded fence. Easy enough to climb up and over. Deeper inside, where better, more effective tech lurked, things wouldn't be so easy.

The luminous cityscape before him grew larger. Towers of dazzling whites and yellows and crimsons, all connected by the weblike latticework of communication spindles, pulsing with the flow of information. A faint golden phosphorescent path appeared before him, leading into the depths of the datasphere and disappearing somewhere inside the dense cluster of structures. His personal yellow brick road, pointing him to the wizard's castle just like in the ancient film. The path's unseen endpoint, which he'd tagged moments earlier on the map, was the human resources department, inside of which he'd find the personnel archives, where he was sure he'd uncover the answers to his questions.

Could it possibly be Gideon? The same Gideon he'd known years ago?

He glided forward, close enough now to spot several intelligent sentries patrolling their routes. Some skittered across the faces of the departmental partitions, visualizing as mechanical insects scurrying across panes of glass. Others darted throughout the empty spaces between the structures, these visualizing as propellerless drones with pellet-shaped robotic bodies and blinking lights. Maddox checked his cloak's status bar. Five percent degradation. Not bad, considering how close he was to the DS's core. Still, though, any degradation at all meant that the ice had begun to melt.

Ten minutes, he guesstimated. That was how long he had, give or take a minute, before active security measures would be able to spot him, setting off every alarm in the DS.

He cautiously moved along his premarked route, entering the datasphere's central cluster of building-like partitions. Moving slowly, he glanced back and forth between his readouts and his surroundings, taking care not to get too close to any of the partition's outer boundaries. He was still cloaked, still functionally invisible, but you never knew what new tech might be embedded in a partition's protective razorwall, lying like a coiled snake hidden in the grass, waiting to strike at any prey passing by. Security analysts loved to tweak razorwall code, modding its capabilities to keep one step ahead of datajackers.

The human resources partition loomed ahead of him, visualizing as a pale blue building with ornate carvings running up and down the corners. Cherubs and angels blowing trumpets, gargoyles perched atop the corners. Maddox stopped a couple clicks from the department's shimmering, opaque razorwall barrier, beyond which information streamed, radiant pulses surging in every direction. Somewhere inside was his target, the archive where the personnel files were stored. He checked the status bar. Ten percent degradation. He was good on time.

Back in the room, a place that now felt a universe away, hands belonging to his meat sack gestured, and in virtual space a modded corkscrew executable appeared before him, visualizing true to its name as a simple magenta spiral.

He took a moment to recheck its settings in a config window, then set it loose on the razorwall. The screw snaked toward the HR partition, a digital viper twisting through virtual space. Maddox watched as it made contact with the razorwall's outer surface, ready to unplug if he caught any signs of detection. The executable paused, its forward tip flush against the razorwall but not penetrating. For a moment Maddox thought something had gone wrong, but then its sidewinding motion began again, and it slowly disappeared inside the partition.

No countermeasures rushed after him. No systemwide lockdown lights flashed, no sirens blared. He checked the cloak's status: eighty-five percent. No increase in its degradation rate. So far so good. Neither he nor the penetrating executable had been detected. Now he simply had to wait for the screw to find personnel archive and, assuming the data leech he'd attached to it worked as planned, retrieve the files he needed.

The waiting was the hardest part. It was a line from some ancient pop song, and Maddox had always thought it apt for moments like these when he found himself deep inside some DS, waiting for an app to complete its instructed task, hoping he'd thought of everything in the code blocks he'd assembled, knowing he probably hadn't. It was impossible to think of everything, to cover every contingency. That was one reason why datajacking wasn't generally a long-term career. Sooner or later, the odds caught up with you, no matter how careful you were. Rooney had been the apparent exception to the rule, the only datajacker Maddox had ever heard of who'd practiced his craft for over twenty years, well into his forties. But then the odds had eventually caught up with him, too, hadn't they?

"Hello, old friend," a voice behind him said.

Maddox whirled his viewpoint around, finding a police badge icon floating half a click in front of him. Back in the room, his hands began to gesture.

"Don't unplug," the voice said quickly.

Maddox paused. He recognized the voice. Gideon.

"Time we had a chat," the badge said, "don't you think?"

Maddox stared at the avatar in disbelief. "Christ, you really are a cop. How did they ever let *you* become a cop?"

Gideon ignored the question. "We can't talk here. Meet me in the cave in ten minutes."

"The cave? You can't be ser—"

"See you there." The badge blinked out and was gone. Maddox gazed at the empty space where it had been a moment before, still stunned by the visitation. Gideon. It was really him. And he was really a cop.

A second later, a warning light flashed red near the bottom of his vision, snapping him out of his funk. The status bar had dropped to ten percent. He quickly began to unplug himself but then stopped.

Gideon. Still cagey as ever. He'd hit Maddox with something that ate away at his cloak like mineral acid through soft rock. Bad, sure, but he could have done much more. He could have frozen Maddox, could have set off systemwide alarms, but he hadn't. Instead, Gideon had hit him with something that would force Maddox out of the DS quickly, while leaving just enough of his cloak intact to do so safely and still undetected.

His old friend didn't want to bust him. At least not at that moment.

Maddox gestured and his avatar sped away from the DS's central cluster, backtracking the path he'd taken moments before. Seconds later he reached the limit of the outermost security perimeter and raced beyond it, still unseen. Safely beyond detection, he watched the status bar disappear as it stopped at two percent.

He hovered there in the ether, his motionless avatar a pinpoint of dull yellow light in an unending virtual universe. He tried to wrap his thoughts around the last few minutes. Had that really just happened? It seemed too insane to believe. Naz Gideon a cop. Here in VS with him.

Maddox knew he should probably unplug. Peel the trodes off his head, break the connection, and figure out the next move once his head stopped spinning.

The cave could be a trap. Likely was a trap. But

then Gideon could have easily trapped him just now in the DS, and he hadn't. Instead, his old acquaintance had simply tapped him on the shoulder.

No small part of Maddox wanted to unplug and catch his breath, knowing that was the prudent move. But however powerful the urge to unplug was, it was diminished by his desperation to unravel the mystery of the mess he was in.

Gideon. Gideon had to have the answers.

Maddox felt his meat sack back in the room take in a deep breath. All right, then. The cave.

10
THE CAVE

Maddox couldn't believe it still existed, but here it was. And here he was, swimming through it.

He raced along the shallow seafloor like a sentient missile, navigating the lesser-known paths through the coral reef as much by memory as sight or his sense of echolocation. The sea was a clear, perfect blue, and from the surface ten meters above his head, dappled sunlight shone down, covering the reef's colorful nodes with a mottled glow. A school of fish, shimmering like a thousand pieces of silver, darted out of his way, exploding out of their tight formation to let him pass through. He recalled how hard it was to catch those little suckers.

When was the last time he'd been a dolphin? Fifteen years ago? More?

The game was called Mantis, and it had been a huge hit back when Maddox had still cared about such diversions. Accessed through specialized gaming specs—or as Maddox was now, through a ported connection to his VS deck—the game put you in the skin of whatever marine life struck your fancy. Killer whale, sea lion, barracuda, tiger shark. Maddox had always preferred the bottlenose dolphin. He'd loved using echolocation, the sound-based sense used by real dolphins and whales for navigation, orientation, even long-distance communication. It was like seeing without eyes, a sensory experience that was impossible to explain to anyone who hadn't played the game.

Mantis had also been his first major datajack. His and Gideon's. The teens had played the game together for countless hours on stolen accounts, fascinated by the environment, a single-instance virtual universe that accurately modeled the breadth and depth of the planet's oceans, less the enormous churning islands of plastic and trash, of course. Together they'd studied leaked source code, uncovering exploits and vulnerabilities. At first they'd used their cheats to level up their aquatic avatars, endowing them with abilities the game designers had never included. Maddox's dolphin could swim at the speed of sound or, if he was in a real rush to get somewhere, teleport. Gideon's mako shark had steel skin and eye lasers.

Later they'd created a secret, untraceable, tightly encrypted location in the game, a cave beneath their favorite reef off the South Pacific coast of New Caledonia. In his old customized avatar, Maddox could have just teleported to the location, but that player account was long gone, auctioned off to some hardcore gamer way back when. In this freeplay skin, he had to get there the old-fashioned way, making the ten-minute swim from a default entry point. The time gave him a chance to gather his thoughts. Or try to, anyway. As he swam along the familiar channels, he still couldn't quite grasp the trajectory of his last couple hours.

Gideon. Their shared history flashed through Maddox's mind as he glided through the warm, sunlit shallows. As teens, the two had first met in Mantis, in these very same virtual waters. And here they'd both been noticed by Rooney, who'd often scouted the gaming feeds for new talent. He'd spotted their rather obvious hacks (teleporting dolphins and steel-skinned sharks were hard to miss in a game that marketed itself as a realistic simulation) and recruited them for his crew. Years later, Maddox had learned his discovery by Rooney had been anything but coincidental. The invisible hand of a now-deceased artificial intelligence had manipulated their lives, making sure Rooney's and his paths had converged to serve its own secret agenda. Maddox pushed those thoughts away, focusing instead on the early days when he and Gideon had first trained as datajackers.

Under Rooney's tutelage, the two learned the ins and outs of core-level virtual space. For the majority of novices, it was an extraordinarily difficult undertaking. The environment required laser-focused concentration and strained the average human brain to the limits of its sensory and cognitive capabilities. Navigating core-level VS was something few could learn, even fewer could master.

Of the two youths, Maddox proved to be the quicker study, becoming Rooney's star pupil, blessed with a preternaturally gifted mind that took to VS like the proverbial fish to water. And while Gideon lacked the other's talent, he bridged the gap with stubborn, single-minded perseverance, slowly but doggedly grinding his way along the learning curve. Where

Maddox succeeded on his first run inside a test environment, Gideon failed a dozen times before finally getting it right. The gap in their respective talents soon proved to be a wedge in their friendship, and what began as a friendly rivalry as gamers deteriorated into a not-so-friendly one as newbie criminals.

About a year into their datajacker careers, Gideon suddenly left Rooney's crew. There one day and gone the next, he disappeared without a word to anyone. And over the nearly two decades since, Maddox had never heard of him again...until today.

He rounded a familiar outcropping of coral, then stopped suddenly as he realized he'd arrived at his destination. Before him was the cave, its small darkened entrance on the seabed between two towering sections of reef. He paused for a few moments. What exactly waited for him down there? Nothing good. He was certain of that much. By the time Gideon had ghosted Rooney's crew, he and Maddox had long since fallen out. Gideon had hated him back then and probably still hated him now. Maddox steeled himself, ready to unplug at any sign of a trap.

He pointed his snout to the cave opening and with a downward sweep of his muscled tail, thrust forward into the darkness...

...and landed on two human feet in the soft sand of the air-filled cave. He checked his avatar, amazed to find the automatic skin switch still worked. His avatar was a fairly accurate replica of his own flesh-and-blood body, dressed in the drab default shirt and trousers the game clothed him in. He looked up at the cave's entrance above his head, the gravity-defying water rippling across it. Incredible, he thought. Their virtual place had survived who knew how many upgrades without getting wiped. Not a bad piece of coding, he mused.

"You're late."

Maddox turned. Gideon stood in a darkened recess at the opposite side of the cave. He stepped out of the shadow into the light filtering down through the water, his gaming skin outfitted in a perfectly tailored suit.

"Can't believe I remembered how to get here," Maddox said. Then, glancing around: "Can't believe this game is still around."

"The community isn't what it used to be," Gideon said, stepping forward. "I suppose enough players hung on to their subscriptions to keep things going."

"You still play?"

"Every now and then. To blow off steam."

"So you're a cop now," Maddox said, shifting topics. "How did that happen?"

"I turned my life around, Blackburn. People change, you know."

"Yeah, I've heard about that," Maddox said. "You find God, too?"

Gideon chuckled. "Not quite."

"How did you find me?"

"Wasn't easy. I had to use just about every trick the old man taught me."

"And how did you know I was in your DS just now?"

Gideon suppressed a grin. "I figured at some point you'd hear my name, want to check my file for yourself. So I put a traffic monitor in the personnel archive, had it ping me if it saw any ripples in the water, so to speak."

Maddox nodded stiffly. "Not bad."

"Thanks."

"So what the hell's going on, Naz?" Maddox asked pointedly. "Why did you want to come here?"

Gideon's mouth tightened into a straight line. "I'm afraid you're in a lot of trouble, Blackburn."

"Tell me something I don't know," Maddox said. "I didn't have anything to do with that bombing over at T-Chen, and you know it."

"Really?" Gideon challenged, lifting his chin skeptically. "So you're saying you *weren't* jacking T-Chen's DS on the very same day their building was bombed?"

Maddox didn't answer.

"And those biker kids we picked up," Gideon continued. "You're telling me they're *not* associates of yours?" He shook his head ruefully. "It doesn't look very good for you right now. Those punks are pretty close to making a confession."

"I bet they are," Maddox said. "How many more shocks you think it'll take?"

"Hard to say," Gideon responded without hesitation. "But they'll get there. And something tells me when they do, one Blackburn Maddox is going to be named as the mastermind behind it all."

Maddox swallowed hard. He was screwed. So very, very screwed.

"You're setting me up," he accused.

"I'm setting you up," Gideon admitted without hesitation, without shame. It was a proud, arrogant reply. He was telling Maddox *I'm a cop and I'm breaking the law and big fucking deal.*

"Care to tell me why?" Maddox asked.

"Because I can, first of all. Christ, Blackburn, you'd be amazed at what you can get away with when you're a cop. But mostly it's because I want to."

Because he wanted to. So that was what this was? Bad blood? An ancient grudge from when they were kids? It was hard to swallow. "A frame-up with fourteen dead bodies. It's a bit overkill for some payback on teenage bullshit, don't you think?"

"Nobody was supposed to get hurt in the bombing. My bad, I guess."

Maddox felt a surge of dread at the lieutenant's casual indifference. What had happened to this man in the years since Maddox had known him that he could shrug off mass murder like some unimportant mishap? Like a ground car's flat tire or an app that crashed in your lenses?

"Nothing ever goes to plan, does it?" Maddox said.

"It's what the old man taught us, right?"

"Yeah, he did." Maddox flicked his wrist and a lit cigarette appear in his hand. The old trick he'd modded still worked, he was relieved to see. He needed a smoke in the worst way.

Maddox inhaled deeply, his mind whirling, at once amazed, troubled, and baffled at the lengths the man had gone to.

"Even without the body count," he said, thinking aloud, "I still don't get it. You've got the whole world in your hands. Why screw that up over little old me? Why go to so much trouble?"

Gideon reached out and touched the cave wall, ran his finger down its moist surface. "Do you remember," he said after a while, "when we got busted and sent to youth detention?"

Maddox remembered. The pair had been arrested trying to market some stolen wares. Through an undercover cop posing as a dealer, as it turned out.

"Sure, I remember," Maddox answered. The overcrowded, understaffed detention facility had been a horrific experience, each day a scrambling, bloody fight for survival.

"Then you probably remember how the old man worked liked crazy to get your time reduced. Called in favors. Made payoffs. Got you out in three months, didn't he? But not me. No, he let me rot in there for a year and a half. Eighteen months in that hellhole. He didn't lift a damn finger to get me out of there."

"That's not true," Maddox argued. "It made him sick that you were in there. I saw it on his face every day. He tried to get you out."

"Sure he did. I bet he tried just as hard as he did with you, didn't he?" He laughed without humor in it. "You know, that time inside taught me some things."

"Like what?"

"Like some people are special. They're born with good looks, or rich parents, or maybe a special talent for datajacking. Those people get treated differently. Doors magically open for them. They get the benefit of every doubt. They get the best jobs, the hottest women. They get their sentences shortened while others stay locked up. They get the best gigs served up on a plate, while others have to fight like street dogs for whatever they can get."

Gideon stepped forward. Maddox felt the long-simmering hatred like heat from an open oven. It leaked from Gideon's avatar like radiation.

"I promised myself a long time ago I'd show you up once and for all, and now I'm finally in a place where I can make it happen." He paused. "And, no, it's not a lot of trouble, Blackburn. Not at all." A demon's smile touched the lieutenant's face. "You're special, after all. You're worth the trouble."

Maddox smoked. "So you brought me here to gloat," he said. "You in your designer suit and me in this thrift shop outfit."

Gideon spread his hands out wide. "A little petty, I admit, but then the best pleasures in life sometimes are. I've been looking forward to this moment for a long time."

"And is it everything you imagined it would be?"

"Oh, yes. And so much more."

The lieutenant's face held the smug satisfaction Maddox had seen a thousand times on the faces of power-tripping cops, highfloor corporati, and underworld crime bosses. It was a look the powerful gave to the powerless. But more than a look, it was an attitude, a warped mindset of those in power who enjoyed ruining lives. Who got off on the suffering of others, especially the helpless and vulnerable.

Maddox took a long draw on his cigarette, smoke filling his lungs. He held the breath for an extended moment before blowing out slowly.

"You know, I was thinking about your career on the way over here," he said. "Thinking about your amazing rise through the ranks. And you know something? It didn't add up."

Gideon appeared amused. "Really? How so?"

"I mean, even for someone as cutthroat as you, making lieutenant before forty? You're barely thirty, same as me. So I was wondering what the hell's the secret sauce here? What does a second-rate datajacker have that got him ahead so quickly?" Maddox gave a mock-surprise look. "And then I realized that was it. Jacking. That's what makes you different."

Gideon's expression darkened at the *second-rate* comment, a reaction Maddox took a small pleasure in.

"So how'd you go about it?" Maddox asked. "You get dirt on your bosses? Dupe their spec feeds when they went to see their mistresses, then blackmail them to bump you up a couple job levels? Or did you fabricate evidence for the higher-ups, digital fingerprints and such, so prosecutors could get some easy convictions on big cases? Christ, you must have been a godsend for some of the old crooks in that precinct building. Of course it was datajacking. That's the only thing that explains it. Because if it were about brains and talent, your career would have peaked at traffic cop."

For a long moment no one spoke. "Same old Blackburn," Gideon finally said through gritted teeth. "Still the smart guy. Still putting together those connections no one else can. Give the man a couple pieces of the puzzle, and he can tell you what the whole damn thing looks like."

"It's a gift," Maddox said, returning smug with smug.

Gideon's hands clenched into fists. "And you still have that smart mouth, don't you? Let's see smart you are with a shockstick up your ass."

"You're never going to get that close to me, you crazy son of a bitch." He took a last drag, dropped his cigarette to the sandy floor of the cave, and unplugged.

11
GOING AWAY PARTY

When the room materialized around Maddox, he found Tommy and Jack leaning forward on the sofa, gazing at him with expectant looks on their faces.

"Well?" Jack asked. "You find what you were looking for?"

And then some, Maddox reflected darkly. He looked around the room with a newfound paranoia. Even though he knew the place was free of listening devices, he still couldn't shake the notion someone might be listening.

"Outside," he said.

The trio stepped through the window onto the fire escape landing, and in the hazy, falling light of early evening, Maddox dropped it on them. After scanning the street for cams and drones and finding none, in hushed tones he told them what had had happened while he was plugged in. What he'd found out and who he'd spoken to.

"Damn, Blackburn," Jack said, whistling in disbelief. "That's one hell of a target you got on your back."

"Yeah, it is," Maddox agreed grimly. A target on his back every cop and street cam and bumblebee drone in the City would be hunting for, probably were already. Standing there in the open air of the fire escape landing, he felt conspicuous and vulnerable, despite the deserted, quiet street below them.

"You got to fight back," Tommy said. "You can't let him get away with it."

"Kid," Maddox said tiredly, "he's already gotten away with it."

"But he's a crook," the kid protested.

"Which makes him no different than any other cop," Maddox said. "Except he's better at it than most."

"You can plug in," the kid pleaded, "find some dirt on him or something, can't you? You say he's been jacking all this time. Maybe find a trail he left behind somewhere."

"Did you hear anything I just said?" Maddox snapped. "He snuck up behind me and tapped me on the shoulder, and I didn't even know he was there. He's a good jacker."

"Good as you?" the kid asked.

"It doesn't matter," Maddox said. "All I know is he's got it in for me, and he's got the law on his side." He took a long drag. "And God knows what he's got looking for me in VS."

The kid's face twisted up in frustration. "And what about my turfies? They're sitting in jail because of this. Because of *you*."

Maddox felt Tommy's anger, his desperation. But the kid didn't appreciate how screwed Maddox was. He didn't know Naz like Maddox did.

"Kid, it was a hell of a setup, watertight. He

probably spent months planning it. And getting set up by a cop is bad enough. But when that cop's a jacker who knows all the ins and outs of our business, all our little tricks we can use to disappear, that's pretty much a nightmare scenario." He shook his head. "There's no fighting back here. There's no counterplay to something like this. With all the cams and drones and tech he has at his fingertips, we're going to be lucky just to get out of the City. Do you understand? It's too bad about your friends. They got a rough break, but there's nothing we can do."

"A rough break?" the kid repeated, glaring. "They're looking at life, jacker. That's not a rough break. That's permanently FUCKED!"

The kid lunged at Maddox in a mad rush, and the datajacker reflexively jerked backward. Before Tommy could take a second step, Jack grabbed him, his huge hands locked around the kid's upper arms. The kid squirmed and struggled uselessly.

"It's all your fault," the kid cried, his voice breaking with emotion. "You owe them, goddammit. You fucking owe them!"

"Take it easy, little brother," Jack said. "Take it easy."

After a few more curses and failed attempts to break free, the kid finally stopped struggling. Jack talked the kid down out of his fit, his voice calm and even, then slowly released his grip. Tommy stood there, breathing heavily. His eyes, welling with tears and boiling with hatred, were locked on Maddox. "You owe them," the kid whimpered.

Maddox didn't say anything. The kid shook his head scornfully, then cursed Maddox in Korean before turning and climbing through the window back into the building.

For a long moment, Maddox stared at the empty space the kid had occupied a moment before. He turned to the rail, leaning with his forearms against the cool metal, his cigarette dangling limply from his lips. He gazed out into the quiet darkness. The brothel's street was deserted, but not entirely. A few businesses operated here and there, oases of light and sound between long stretches of crumbling, gutted husks of lowrises. The nearest such oasis was a Thai food joint a couple blocks down, its molded plastic tables spilling out onto the sidewalk and crowded with patrons.

"Nothing I can do," Maddox muttered, more to himself than Jack.

"Maybe not," Jack said. "He's a young pup, Blackburn. Still got a lot to learn. He'll see it straight when he cools down some. Don't you worry."

"Who said I was worried?"

For a long moment neither man spoke. The din from the Thai joint rose from the street, a murmuring buzz of conversation and laughter.

"So what *are* you going to do?" Jack asked, finally breaking the silence.

Maddox blew smoke. "I don't know yet," he replied honestly.

"Going to leave the City?"

"Probably have to." Maddox knew a thousand places to hide in the City. But they were the kinds of places a datajacker could hide for a week or two, maybe a month, until the heat died down. But heat like this didn't die down, ever. The cops didn't just let corporate terrorists skate away. They tracked them down, aggressively and tirelessly, like the corporations wanted them to. Hell, T-Chen Engineering would probably even hire out a crew of mercenaries to join the hunt. Gideon had played the whole thing to perfection.

"Guess there's only one thing we can do, then," Jack said, laying a heavy hand on Maddox's shoulder.

Maddox glanced at him. "What's that?"

The fighter cocked his head toward the window. "Have a little going away party…on me."

Maddox looked over. The modded woman he'd seen earlier stood just inside the window, gazing at him naughtily and holding her vest open wide, her four perfect breasts pressed against the glass.

Same old Jack. Any excuse for a party. Under any conditions.

Maddox looked at the woman as he pondered the uncertain path he'd been dropped onto. Going forward, his life would be one of endless running and hiding and looking over his shoulder. These next few hours might be the last stretch of relative peace he was going to have for a long while. He flicked his cigarette off the landing and figured what the hell.

Might as well spend those hours doing something interesting.

12
VIP EXIT

"You really a datajacker, honey?" the woman asked. She leaned forward, her pinkish muscled thighs pressed against the vanity, her face close to the mirror as she dabbed a fresh sheen of lipstick onto her mouth. "That's what Celeste says." As she spoke, a little circle of fog appeared on the glass in front of her mouth.

"Used to be," Maddox answered. He lay on the bed, still catching his breath, the sheets warm and wrinkled and vaguely damp beneath his back.

The naked woman—Maddox realized he hadn't caught her name—turned toward him, her four breasts softly bobbing. When he'd first seen this particular mod, he'd been put off by the oddness of it, but now…

"I'm up here, honey," the woman droned, pointing to her face. Maddox lifted his gaze to meet her eyes, self-consciously realizing she'd asked him a second question he hadn't registered.

"Sorry, what did you say?"

"My little boy's gaming deck?" she said, apparently

repeating herself. "You think you can fix it? He threw a fit about losing ten levels or some nonsense and tossed the thing across the room. Now he can't get it to turn on."

Maddox reached for his shirt, fished around the pockets for a smoke. "Don't really know much about the hardware side of things," he lied. "Not sure I could help much."

The woman strapped herself into a four-cupped bra. "Probably just as well. He's on that thing too much anyway. Like that kid you came with."

Maddox gave up the search for a smoke. "Tommy? He's still here?"

She motioned to the ceiling. "Two floors up with Ginger."

Maddox lifted his eyebrows. "I guess he wasn't that upset after all, then."

"Upset about what?"

"Long story. He read me the riot act earlier. Now he's up there getting laid. Seems like he bounced back pretty quick."

"Getting laid nothing," she said dismissively. "That boy's up there playing around on Ginger's deck."

Maddox froze. Had he heard her right? "Did you say playing on a deck?"

The woman shrugged. "Said he wanted to plug into some game. Asked me which girl had the best gear."

"I thought you were off-grid here."

"We are," she said, stepping into her skirt. "That's what I told him. I said, 'Ginger has gaming gear, hon, but you won't be able to…'"

No longer listening, Maddox dressed in a frenzied

rush, jumping into his pants and pulling his shirt over his head. What the hell was the kid trying to do, get them all caught? The scramble shields might keep *this* building off the grid, but if the kid really wanted to plug in, all he had to do was hop over to the next roof with a deck and a remote link. Or if he found a gap in the coverage, he might only have to go out onto the fire escape.

Maddox bolted from the room and up two flights of stairs. Pounding on a succession of locked doors, he called out for Tommy. "You in there, kid? Let me in."

At the end of the hallway, the last door on the left opened. A young woman's face, pale-skinned with red bangs hanging to her eyes, tentatively peeked out. Ginger, apparently. "What do you want with him?"

Maddox ran over. The redhead yelped in surprise as he shouldered his way into the room. He searched the cramped, dimly lit space. Empty bed and a tiny end table wedged next to the wall.

"The hell, man?" the woman said, annoyed. "Hit me in the face with the fucking door next time." The room was barely big enough for the two of them.

"Where is he?"

"Out there," she said, gesturing to the window. Red velvet drapes hung to the floor, billowing in the breeze. Beyond them, Maddox spied Tommy sitting on a plastic chair, hunched over a deck and gesturing with his hands.

Maddox bodily moved the woman out of his way and sidestepped through the tight space between the foot of the bed and the wall. At the window, he pulled open the drapes and leaned out, reaching for the trodes on Tommy's head. The kid's eyes were closed and his hands were a few centimeters above the deck strapped to his lap. He was in mid-gesture when Maddox ripped the trodes off.

"Hey," the kid cried, his tone like he'd been caught jerking off. His hands rose quickly to his temples, and his eyes jumped around unfocused. It took him a second or two to shake off the disorientation, and when he did, his expression went from recognition to annoyed in a millisecond.

"What are you doing, pulling me out like that?" the kid said.

"What am *I* doing?" Maddox shot back. "We're here to stay off the radar. What the hell are *you* doing is the question. That didn't look like a gaming gesture to me."

The kid glared at Maddox. He'd been caught red-handed, but he clearly didn't care. A standby icon floated above the deck. The kid tossed the device onto the bed.

"Thanks for the loan, Ginger," he called.

Maddox stepped out onto the fire escape. He scowled down at the kid. "What were you doing?"

"Trying to help my friends," Tommy snapped. "Since nobody else around here will."

"Trying to help them how?" Maddox pressed.

The kid broke eye contact, shifted in his seat.

"Help them how?" Maddox repeated.

"Figured if I, you know," he said, fidgeting, "get some dirt on that cop, might be able to cut a deal with him, get him to call the dogs off."

Maddox swallowed hard. "Tell me you didn't just try to jack the police department."

"Never got that far," Tommy admitted. "You pulled me out while I was still shopping apps."

"Kid, listen to me. You can't plug in. *At all.* Not even for a game. They're looking for us. You understand that?"

"But if I'm cloaked, can't I—"

"No, you can't," Maddox interrupted. "And I'll tell you why. Because we're at the top of the wanted list. And when you're that famous, they throw military-grade tech at you. Then all the normal rules go right out the window. Between the local cops and the feds, they've probably got three or four AIs hunting us. A cloaking app's useless against that kind of search. It's like a raincoat, kid. You might have a good one that keeps you dry in the worst storm, but it won't do jack to protect you from a nuclear bomb. And that's where we are right now. Different game, different rules."

The kid met Maddox's gaze. "But you one-upped an AI before. I was there when you did it."

"That was a once-in-a-lifetime trick, and we had a good amount of luck on our side." Not to mention another AI, he added internally. "You don't pull that kind of thing off a second time."

Tommy's face hardened. "I'm not going to run and hide. And I'm not going to sit on my hands. Those are my turfies, jacker."

Maddox threw his hands up. He'd had enough of the kid and his tribal drama. "You want to get yourself arrested, go right ahead. Throw yourself right into the meat grinder for all I care. Just do it someplace far from me, got it?"

He turned to the window and started to duck back into the building when something caught his eye down on the street. He stood back up, peering into the darkness beyond the Thai joint. Aside from the abandoned husk of an old hover, there was nothing there. Maybe his newly paranoid state was messing with him, but he thought he'd seen movement a few blocks—

The customers at the restaurant shrieked, then scattered in all directions, toppling chairs and tables in a frantic rush. Maddox crouched and quickly donned his specs. He scanned the area, seeing nothing at first. Then after a moment, he managed to pick out the faint silhouettes of figures with guns, nearly invisible, moving slowly toward the building. Cops in chameleon armor. Maddox swung his vision in the opposite direction. Five blocks down, a second group approached, wearing the same adaptive gear that rendered its wearers nearly invisible. Maddox swallowed. Feds, he thought grimly. Only Feds wore adaptive armor.

The faint whine of a hover motor grew quickly louder. The overlay on Maddox's specs lit up as its audio filters recognized the vehicle's engine signature. POLICE HOVER INBOUND flashed wildly in the lower portion of his lens. An instant later, the modifier MULTIPLE appeared.

A hand grabbed him by the upper arm. He whirled around to find Jack.

"Time to go," he said. "Roof cams picked up cop hovers coming our way."

Maddox scrambled back inside. "I saw two Fed SWAT teams on the street," he told the fighter.

"Just gets better and better," Jack said, waving Tommy inside. "Come on, little brother."

Pausing in the doorway, Maddox called to Jack. "Screw the kid. He's the one who plugged in and brought them down on us."

"Did not," the kid protested. "Nobody saw me, I swear."

Outside, the motor whine was now an ear-piercing shriek as several hovers made hurried landings on the surrounding roofs and streets. The trio scrambled into the hallway and Jack led them to the stairwell. The din from the engines died down, enough for Maddox to hear breaking glass and shouts and screams coming up from the ground floor. The raid had begun.

"Tenth floor," Jack hollered, holding the door and waving them into the stairwell. Maddox noticed a gun in the fighter's hand as he and Tommy ran past.

Up, turn, up, turn. They ran up the flights, bounding two and three stairs at a time. "What's on ten?" Maddox shouted to Jack.

"There's a bridge to the next building for VIPs," Jack called as they reached the eighth-floor landing. "Then down to the basement. Connects to a subway service tunnel."

A VIP exit. Brothels often had them for anyone who needed a more discreet way in and out of the place than simply walking in off the street. People in the public eye, mostly. Actors, politicians, Wall Street wizards. The types who didn't want to risk even the slightest tarnish to their public image.

"POLICE! STAY WHERE YOU ARE!"

The amplified voice blared from somewhere above them. Maddox risked an upward glance as he reached the ninth floor. Four flights above, half a dozen cops raced down toward them.

The first shots rang out as they reached the tenth floor, pinging off the metal handhold, sending sparks flying. The crack of automatic gunfire reverberated off the stairwell's concrete walls, magnifying the sound and assaulting their ears. Maddox flinched but kept running. He threw open the door and burst into the tenth-floor hallway, followed by Tommy and Jack.

"Where?" Maddox asked, panting, his heart thudding in his chest.

"She said room ten-two-two," Jack answered, pointing the way.

Tommy reached the room first, shouldering through the door. Maddox followed close behind, then stopped short at what he saw. Jack brought up the rear, thudding into Maddox as he entered the small, empty room.

"How are we supposed to go across *that*?" the kid asked.

The VIP corridor—less a corridor than the barest idea of one—was a partially constructed nanocrete structure, two meters in diameter, connecting the room's window and its neighbor in the next building, some seven meters away. Its construction had never been completed, or it had been recently damaged. Either way, to Maddox it looked like a disintegrating tunnel sagging precariously in the air ten stories above the street. The metal framework, thin and rusted and spindly-looking, was visible in several areas where there should have been at least a couple inches of solid nanocrete. The thing looked like a death trap.

Outside the room, the stairwell door opened with a telltale bang against the wall. A metallic amplified voice barked an order to search the floor room by room.

"We got to go one at a time," Jack said. "Go on, little brother. Carefully, now."

The kid didn't need to be told twice. He tiptoed

through the tunnel, his hands pressed gingerly against the walls. He moved quickly but carefully, like a person trying to find the least searing path through a bed of burning coals. The structure sagged and quivered. Chunks of nanocrete broke away and fell to the alley floor far below. From the hallway, the sound of doors being kicked open grew louder as the kid reached the other side and hopped safely into the opposite room.

"Your turn," Jack said. "Go on."

"You go," Maddox said. "Give me the gun. I'll hold them off."

Jack shook his head. "My big ass won't get halfway across that rickety thing."

"It'll hold," Maddox insisted. He heard the sound of another doorway getting kicked in behind them.

"Fine, fine," Jack said. The fighter held out the gun for Maddox, but as the other reached for it, Jack snatched it away and grabbed Maddox by the wrist and twisted his arm behind his back. Before Maddox could protest, Jack was shoving him toward the window.

"No time to argue," Jack grunted as he thrust Maddox headlong into the tunnel. "Get out of here, VIP."

Maddox tumbled, coming to a sprawling stop in the middle of the flimsy structure. The framework sagged under his weight and felt as if it would break apart. He scrambled forward on all fours, expecting the tunnel to open up under him at any moment and send him plunging to the hard ground. Then, somehow, he was through. Tommy's hands were on him, pulling him out of the death trap and into the room.

The skies opened up and a hard rain began to fall as Maddox turned and looked across the gap between the buildings. Jack stood on the other side, framed by the window. Maddox waved him forward.

"Come on!"

The fighter climbed onto the windowsill and tossed the gun through the air in a gentle arc. Maddox caught it and shoved it into the back of his pants.

Jack paused, looking at the structure doubtfully. "I hate heights, Blackburn. You know that, right?" Raindrops pelted the fighter's head and shoulders.

Behind Jack, the room's door flew open. Maddox watched as the next few moments passed with agonizing slowness. Jack scrambled into the tunnel and it immediately collapsed. The side connected to the building opposite Maddox fell away. The metal framework on Maddox's side bent and twisted as the passageway broke in half, one part plummeting to the alley, the other still partially connected and hanging precariously against the building's side. The broken section hit the ground with a thud, the metal framework flattened under the weight of the nanocrete.

Maddox leaned out the window and peered downward. Amazingly, Jack was there, clutching onto the bent framework with one hand, the building ledge with the other.

"I could use a hand, Blackburn," he said, grimacing a smile and struggling to keep his grip. Around him, the broken remains of the tunnel made metallic popping sounds as it began to sheer away.

Maddox reached down and grabbed the fighter around the wrists. Gunfire blazed out of the opposite window and Jack stiffened, his eyes going wide.

"I'm shot," the fighter grunted. "I'm shot."

The last connections of the tunnel's framework snapped under the strain of the heavy load and fell away, nearly taking Jack with it as it tumbled to the ground. Jack hung alongside the building, his eyes still wide with shock and disbelief.

Maddox pulled, his back straining, but Jack was heavy and his arms were slick with rain. Maddox couldn't keep his grip.

"Jack, swing your feet onto the ledge!"

More gunfire. Maddox winced as things popped and exploded around him. He felt Jack's body shiver, then the fighter's grip went slack and blood oozed from his mouth.

"Jack!"

The fighter's eyes glazed over. "Take little brother and get out of here, Blackburn," he said, spitting blood.

And then he slipped away, a slow tumble downward in the falling rain. Maddox yelled the fighter's name again and watched his friend fall, yanking his eyes away an instant before Jack struck the ground.

13
LONG TIME NO SEE

Later, Maddox would only recall the immediate aftermath of Jack's death as a blur of disconnected moments he'd navigated in a dull stupor. A vague recollection of Tommy taking the gun and firing back at the cops. The kid pulling him out of the room and down to the basement. The two of them making it to the subway and riding the 7 train to the end of the line, then hunkering down in an abandoned shopping center in Flushing.

When Maddox finally recovered his wits, he ripped into the kid.

"You killed him, you damned fool," he sneered. "You might as well have put a bullet in his head."

The kid tried to defend his actions, but Maddox wasn't hearing any of it. "You plugged in and ten minutes later the cops are up our asses. They tagged you, just like I said they would."

"But I was cloaked," the kid shot back, "there's no way they could have—"

"How the fuck would you know?" Maddox interrupted. "You're not a datajacker. You're a wannabe. How many times have you plugged into core VS? Five? Six? And half of those times I was there holding your hand. You've got blind spots as big as whole galaxies. You got Jack killed tonight, you little shit."

Something seemed to break inside the kid, snapping like a dry twig. He cast his eyes down at his shoes. "I just wanted to help my friends," he said somberly. "I didn't think—"

"No, you didn't think," Maddox said, "as usual."

They stood there for a long moment in silence. Rainwater dripped from the roof into a puddle on the cracked tile floor. Tommy sat, still staring downward. The kid's head hung low, his shoulders rounded in defeat, as if the scolding had beaten him down physically. Or maybe it was simply exhaustion, Maddox thought, aware of his own overwhelming tiredness. The comedown crash following an hours-long adrenaline rush.

The kid removed his jacket, balled it up for a pillow, and lay down with his back to Maddox.

"They're my friends," he whimpered.

Maddox sat, blew out a long breath. "I know, kid." He wanted to say more, but no words came.

Yes, the kid had screwed up. Screwed up badly. But this whole thing wasn't the kid's mess, Maddox reminded himself. And when he could have kept Jack out of it, Maddox hadn't pushed hard enough. So if there was blame to be assigned for Jack's death, Maddox confessed inwardly that a large portion of it—if not the entire share—belonged to him.

Moments later, Tommy dozed off. Maddox watched as the kid slept, snoring lightly. He shouldn't have blown up at the kid like that. Rooney had never given him a tongue-lashing like that, even when the younger version of himself had fully earned it.

In the morning he'd set things right. More than most, Maddox knew what death-guilt could do to a person, and he didn't want Tommy to suffer as he had, haunted by a pain and regret that never went away.

Overcome with fatigue, Maddox lay down on the cold, hard floor. Sleep came almost instantly, less a conscious decision than a helpless surrender.

When he awoke a few hours later, Tommy was gone.

*   *   *

Regret. It was something datajackers didn't deal with often. Regret was for the unsure, the indecisive. Regret was a rearview mirror that drew your attention away from the present, from the problems at hand. A keen sense of the present, of the now, was a trait common among the best datajackers. They were masters of the moment. Rooney had shared this observation with Maddox early in his apprenticeship. It wasn't necessarily an inability to feel regret, or nostalgia, or any other backward-looking emotion, Rooney had explained. It was instead an innate compulsion to keep things moving forward, for not allowing the past to be an anchor that held you back, that slowed you down. If a shark stops swimming it dies, Maddox had once heard. Elite datajackers were much the same way.

But not always. Rooney's death was the one thing he'd never been able to move completely past. Without fail, it seeped into his everyday thoughts and actions, tugging at what Maddox supposed was a conscience. The questions would always come. Why hadn't he heeded the little voice nagging at him, telling him something was wrong long before they'd plugged in? Why hadn't he insisted that Rooney bail on that gig that had ultimately taken his life?

Maddox sat up, groggy and dry-throated from the cold night air, his back aching from the hard floor. A haze of predawn light entered the empty space from a broken window high up the far wall. He rolled a cigarette, his fingers moving automatically as he blinked himself awake. He'd been dreaming of Rooney's final days.

He lit the tip, blew smoke. Maybe the dream had to do with the kid. Maddox regretted berating Tommy, hanging Jack's death around the kid's neck, and one regret in the conscious world had triggered another in the dream world. And now the kid was gone. Maddox sat there smoking, forgetting the regret of his dreams, remorseful only about the last words he'd spoken to Tommy. He might never see the kid again, might never have the chance to tell him it wasn't his fault. He might have cursed the kid for life, throwing an unbearable weight upon his soul.

But as shitty as Maddox felt about it, it didn't change his current lot. He was still a wanted man, still had to get out of the City. He stood on stiff legs, stretched, and tried to wall off the regret or guilt or whatever it was he'd awoken to this morning.

The next few hours would be his last in the City. If he wanted to be gone by noon, he had no time to waste.

*   *   *

The little drone waited patiently in the air conditioning vent, watching the room through the vent cover's horizontal slits. The drone had been sitting in this very spot for months, unmoving and fully powered down to conserve its battery life, awaiting the signal from its master to awaken. Today, the signal had finally come.

It watched the room for a long while, its egg-shaped body and three pairs of spiderlike legs quiet and unmoving, unable to begin its task until the room was empty. Two men moved about in the room. They talked with each other in low tones, turning over sofa cushions and opening drawers. They were looking for something and, apparently, not finding it. Clothes and pillows and the contents of drawers lay strewn about the floor. After what seemed like a very long time to the little drone, the men stopped searching and left, ducking under the wide yellow tape across the door that said POLICE SCENE DO NOT ENTER. Before they closed the door, the drone noticed two other people, both holding rifles and dressed in police armor, standing on either side of the door.

When the room was empty, the drone waited another ten minutes—its master had programmed it to have a cautious nature—before it began to remove the screws of the vent cover. It did its job with admirable precision, making sure each screw came out silently so the guards couldn't hear. The trickiest part was removing the vent cover and sliding it back into the shaft, but this too the little drone performed to perfection, making not the slightest sound.

Freed from its hiding place, the drone opened its carapace and unfurled its four wings. The men hadn't left behind any cameras or audio bugs—it had been watching and scanning for such devices every time someone had entered—so it skipped over the parts of its instructions that dealt with disabling police gadgets. Revving its wings to a fast spin, it dropped from the air vent into the room like a rock, then stopped halfway to the floor. It rotated in place, taking one last scan—cautious, cautious, cautious—and finding no devices. The drone then flew back into its hiding place and reappeared moments later, carrying a canvas bag in its legs. This was its precious cargo, its reason for existence. It held the heavy bag tight to its body, wings humming softly as it floated to the window. The window had instructions, too, and it slid open a few centimeters, just enough for the little drone and its valuable load to escape the only home it had ever known.

From the roof of a nearby building, Maddox watched the window of his condo, his vision magnified through his specs. Where was the thing? He'd remotely kicked off the routine half an hour ago. The hornet drone he'd hidden in his apartment should have shown itself by now. No, that wasn't right, he corrected himself, recalling the code he'd written into the drone's memory months earlier. If there were anyone present in the unit—especially cops—it would wait until they left. And then after that, to keep its existence and, more importantly, its cargo secret, it would have to disable any monitoring devices the cops had left behind.

Then he saw the window crack open, and a moment later the little drone emerged, carrying the bag. He blew out in relief. Good.

It took a few more minutes for the drone to reach Maddox, who was only a few blocks away but across several transit lanes. The drone navigated the hazardous skyways, then delivered its load to its owner. Maddox opened the bag, counted the bills, and stuffed them into his jacket pocket. All right, that was the last one.

He'd spent the morning collecting cash at multiple stashes he had around the City. Some were in storage lockers rented under a fake ID. Those were the quickest and easiest to retrieve. All he had to do was show up with the key. Others weren't so quick, like the cigar box of cash he'd left inside a hidden nook in a parking garage. He'd committed the address of the place to memory, but he'd forgotten which floor. Cursing himself repeatedly, he'd spent over an hour before he finally found what he was looking for. He'd deemed his apartment as the riskiest, most complex pickup, so he'd left it for last. And now he was finished. His pockets were stuffed with enough cash to get him far away from the City.

Time to get out of town.

He took the stairwell down to the ground level, opened a door, and emerged into the alley.

"Salaryman," a voice said from behind him. He whirled around.

"Long time no see," the woman said.

Beatrice. Wait, Beatrice? He stared at her, blinking. He hadn't seen the mercenary woman in over a year, since they'd both tangled with the Latour-Fisher AI. She was the last person in the world he expected to see at that moment. Recovering from his surprise, Maddox noticed she hadn't changed since their last meeting. Her hair still had the same short-cropped cut, dyed blond with dark roots. She still wore the simple garb that looked thrown together from discount bins, an unremarkable, easily forgettable ensemble—black jeans and a loose jacket over a formfitting sky-blue T-shirt—an outfit designed to blend in with the street-level crowds. Oversized specs with dark lenses covered the top half of her face, concealing most of her expression save the tight grin. Without seeing her eyes, Maddox wasn't sure if the smile she was giving him was a good one or the other kind.

"What are you doing—" He cut himself off as his eyes drifted downward and spotted the Ruger in her right hand, half-hidden by the jacket sleeve.

The smile was still there when he looked back up at her face. It wasn't the good kind, he decided.

"We need to talk," she said.

14
A MERCENARY'S DEBT

"How'd you find me?" Maddox asked, tapping a neat line of tobacco from his bag and rolling up the rice paper.

"Still smoking, I see," Beatrice said with a disapproving frown. He knew from their previous partnership she had a special aversion toward this particular vice. Maybe that was why he felt a tiny bit of pleasure—aside from the nicotine rush—as he lit the tip and inhaled.

"Seriously, how?" he asked, blowing smoke.

They sat in a lavishly furnished fiftieth-floor apartment in Midtown, the sole occupants of the unit. The windows were darkened—you never know who might be watching—and a single floor lamp provided the room's dim, long-shadowed illumination. A ceiling fan turned slowly overhead, dissipating the ribbons of smoke that rose from Maddox's cigarette.

Beatrice stared at him dully, gave half a shrug. "You're good at what you do, I'm good at what I do. Let's leave it at that."

"This your place?" Maddox asked, looking around.

"It is today," she said vaguely.

Maddox blew smoke. "If you wanted to talk, you didn't have to pull a gun on me, you know."

A hint of a smile touched her lips. "I didn't pull it on you. I was just holding it. Whatever you inferred from that is your business, salaryman."

The last time he'd seen Beatrice, he'd actually entertained the notion that he'd grown fond of her. Thought perhaps she'd entertained the same notion. But here and now, those moments seemed like someone else's life, lived a long time ago.

He flicked ash onto the hardwood floor. "What do you want?"

"I was in Toronto on a job when I saw the news about the bombing and who got arrested for it. Thought you might know something, so I tracked you down." She explained how she'd been a block away from his building when she'd spotted a huddle of rhino cops, chattering with each other like they were getting ready for a raid. Warning bells going off in her head, she'd backed off and released a handful of bumblebee drones to watch the building. One of them had spotted Maddox's drone leaving the condo, and that had led her straight to him.

"Call me a skeptic," she said, "but I'm not buying this terrorist story. You lot never struck me as the political types."

"Oh, but we are," Maddox said. "I love sticking it to the man, and those kids are my faithful minions. Long live the revolution." He held up a mocking fist.

"Still smoking, and still a smartass," she said. "So what is it, then? What's the story? You got an AI after you again, spinning lies about you and those kids?"

"I wish." He blew smoke, wanting to leave his

answer at that. But the look on her face said she wasn't letting him out of her sight until her questions were answered.

"Somebody on the police force has it in for me," he confided.

"I kind of figured most cops did," she quipped.

"This is different."

"Personal beef?"

"You're getting warmer," he said.

Beatrice listened raptly as he recounted the strange story of the last few days, a sequence of events he still had trouble grasping himself. He cursed himself again for failing to uncover the sham gig with Sanchez. It was the same kind of mistake Rooney had made, taking on that fatal gig too quickly, too eagerly, his vision clouded by the dollar signs in his eyes. His old mentor had paid the ultimate price for his mistake. Maddox wondered bleakly if he'd bought himself the same ticket.

"And the Anarchy Boyz?" Beatrice asked.

"Known associates," he answered, then added, "with a recent history of helping me evade arrest, if you recall." Maybe they'd been brought in, he explained, simply because Gideon had wanted to grill them, find out if they knew Maddox's whereabouts. Or maybe they'd been part of the setup plan all along, the foundation of a convenient, easily concocted storyline that painted the kids as corporate terrorists and Maddox as their evil puppet master.

He took a long drag on his cigarette. The story, he knew, had to sound crazy. But oddly, as he related it, Beatrice didn't react, and if she doubted any part of the wild tale, she gave no indication. She simply sat there, detached and contemplative, taking it all in.

When he finished, she nodded slowly. "So all of this is a frame-up to get you out of the way?"

Maddox nodded, blew smoke. "Quite the mess, isn't it?"

"Seems like a lot of trouble to go to, don't you think?"

"That's exactly what I said."

"So why not just put a bullet in you if he's so hot to bring you down?"

"Because he doesn't want me dead. Not yet, anyway. He wants to ruin me first, humiliate me in front of the world, and in the process make sure everyone knows it was him who got the better of me."

"Jesus, salaryman," Beatrice said, "you sure bring out the best in people, don't you?"

"It's a gift."

"So what now?"

Maddox smoked. "What do you mean?"

"What's your next move?"

He looked at her crossly. "Well, let's see. I've got every cop in the City looking for me, some feds too, and probably half a dozen government AIs on top of that. I'm thinking getting the hell out of here is the way to go."

"You're leaving?"

"Of course I am."

"When?"

"Now."

"So you're just going to bail on those kids?" Beatrice asked pointedly.

Maddox snorted. "I'm not bailing on anybody. There's nothing I can do for them."

"That's bullshit."

Christ, she sounded like Tommy. "You know what's bullshit?" He blew smoke. "You thinking I can do anything about the mess they're in."

"Come on," she scoffed, "this whole thing sounds like a house of cards waiting to come down. And if you weren't so busy trying to save your own ass, you'd see it."

"A house of cards?"

"Think about it," she said. "This Gideon can't be pulling off this frame-up on his own, can he? It's too big. It's got too many moving parts. Whoever he's pulled into this mad little revenge plot with him has to be sweating bullets right about now, worried the feds or the higher-ups in the department will find out, or God forbid, some reporter pieces it all together. People make careers out of uncovering scandals like this. This old friend of yours is taking a huge gamble."

Thoughts along these lines had already occurred to him. Gideon had been a gambler his whole life. Beatrice had that part figured out. Maddox had never known him to play things safe, always going all in. Why punch someone in the nose when you can crush them into a bloody pulp? That was who he was.

Still, even if Gideon's scheme was a house of cards, Maddox was powerless to kick it down. His old datajacking colleague simply had too many weapons at his disposal. Pushing back was pointless, doomed to failure.

When Maddox didn't respond, Beatrice went on. "Let me put it another way. What's the first thing that happens if our bad lieutenant is out of the picture? His buddies down at the precinct get busy making sure the whole stinking mess goes away quickly and quietly."

"Yeah," Maddox agreed, "by locking those kids up at Rikers and throwing away the key."

"No, by letting them off."

Maddox chuckled darkly. "Maybe in some parallel universe, sister, where fair is fair and people never go down for crimes they don't commit. But here in the City, the wheels of justice don't exactly turn that way."

He'd heard enough. He started to leave, his attention already shifting elsewhere as he mentally mapped out ways to get out of Manhattan undetected. Beatrice sprang up from the sofa and grabbed his arm.

"There's got to be something we can do," she insisted.

"Look," he sighed, "maybe I don't entirely disagree with you on this house of cards notion. Maybe if Naz were out of the picture, things might fall apart. Maybe they'd even cut those kids loose, who knows? But it's not like we can just take him down, now is it? It's one thing to say it. Doing it, that's something else. We'd never get close enough."

"Nobody's untouchable," she said.

"Wanna bet?"

Her gaze didn't waver. "I owe those kids, Blackburn. Maybe that makes me old-school. Maybe it makes me weak. If it does, so fucking be it. All I know is I'm not going to sit around and do nothing while they go down like this."

He gently removed her hand from his arm. "I'm sorry," he insisted. "I can't."

A long moment passed between them.

"Fine," she said, gesturing. "There's the door."

On the end table, her specs began to vibrate, an

alert box flashing on the lens. She held them up in front of her face, reading whatever was there.

"Goddammit," she muttered, shaking her head in disbelief. She let out a long, tired breath. "They arrested Tommy. It's all over the news feeds."

Maddox removed his own lenses from his shirt collar and put them on, pulling up a news feed. Sure enough, there was Tommy goddamn Park, being pulled out of a cop hover, hands cuffed and surrounded by a crush of media reporters and camera drones. A throng of cops hustled him through the crowd and up the steps into the Ninth Precinct building.

ANOTHER BOMBING SUSPECT APPREHENDED, the scrolling headline read.

* * *

Maddox leaned forward with his forearms on the fire escape, the rail's metal cool against his skin. Fifty stories below the City thrummed, bright and bustling, its avenues teeming. The clogged neon arteries of some giant organism. At this height traffic thinned out considerably, reduced to a scattering of shiny expensive vehicles shuttling the highfloor wealthy among the City's superstructure mountains. He blew smoke, alone with his thoughts, the quiet broken only by the occasional whine of a passing hover.

Bad decisions. Life was full of them. Sometimes you made them knowingly, striding confidently forward and then smashing your face into the brick wall your little voice had warned you would be there. Then other times you were clueless, turning right on a whim when you should have gone left, utterly ignorant of your mistake, unaware of the uncovered manhole you were about to step into. Bad decisions.

He'd certainly made his fair share, knowingly and otherwise.

Don't we all, boyo?

Wonderful. Perfect. Not a word for months, now Rooney picked this moment to pop back into his head.

It was hopeless, Maddox insisted, both to himself and to the ghost of his old mentor. Naz had eyes and ears everywhere. Even with the help of Beatrice's two expert hands, Maddox was outgunned, outmanned, outeverythinged. He wasn't even sure he could make it out of the City in one piece. And as much as he wanted to fry Gideon in hot oil, as much as he was bothered by the idea of Tommy and his turfies doing hard time, contemplating anything beyond his own survival was unthinkable right now. Undoable. Thoroughly unwise.

He gazed down at the City's ceaseless churn, unable to lose himself in its countless distractions, unable to shake the news feed image of Tommy in cuffs, the kid's eyes wide and frightened.

You didn't leave me in that prison we shared, did you, boyo?

I was trapped there, just like you were. Don't you remember?

But if you could, would you have?

No.

Then why are you leaving now?

Maddox didn't answer, his gaze still fixed on the floor of the City.

Jack could have left you, boyo, but he didn't.

And look what had happened to him.

Maddox squeezed his eyes shut until he was sure the voice in his head had been silenced. He opened them again and took a long pull on his cigarette. Holding in the smoke for a long moment, he thought of Jack. Foolish, loyal Jack. He blew out again.

That kid. He's going to be the end of me.

The voice in his head returned, laughing. *Boyo, if you only knew how many times I said the same thing.*

Maddox turned to Beatrice. The mercenary sat in the window, her back against the sill.

"You wouldn't happen to have a deck and trode set, would you?" he asked.

She lifted an eyebrow. "Change of plans?"

"Yeah," he said.

She grinned, nodded her approval. "Top shelf of the closet. White box."

Bad decisions, bad decisions. He'd made his fair share.

Add another one to the list.

15
SPECIAL AGENT NGUYEN

Moments after he walked through the door, Deke's hands were damp with a cold sweat. No accusations had been hurled, no other shoe had dropped. Not yet, anyway. He did his best to hide the stress from his face, smiling through the introductions and small talk about the special agent's flight into Manhattan and the unseasonably warm weather.

It was the man's look that unnerved Deke. Special Agent Alex Nguyen had a definite look about him, sitting there with his perfectly tailored suit and wire-rimmed spectacles. His meticulous manner, his precise way of speaking. This was an intelligent man, a thorough man, a man who missed nothing. He was exactly the kind of man Deke imagined would bust him and the lieutenant.

Five minutes earlier, Deke and Gideon had been summoned to the special agent's fifth-floor office. Nguyen had just been put on the T-Chen bombing case, settling into a borrowed precinct office that same morning after arriving on an early flight from D.C., then spending the next few hours reviewing the case files. The F.B.I. assigned a federal liaison to every suspected terrorist crime in the City. Standard procedure. Deke had been dreading this moment, the first meeting between him, the lieutenant, and the special agent. He'd known it was coming and he and the lieutenant had planned for it, but still he felt woefully unprepared.

Gideon sat next to Deke, looking relaxed and amiable, as if he were lunching with an old acquaintance. If his boss felt any of the gut-twisting anxiety Deke did, he'd managed to conceal it behind a perfect mask of calm and ease.

When the agent's call came, Gideon had made it quite clear he didn't want Deke doing any of the talking. Don't offer up anything, don't speak unless spoken to, the lieutenant had instructed him. And if asked anything by Nguyen, the detective was to play dumb. Deke was to say he'd been focused only on coordinating their men in the field, organizing the search for suspects. He knew little about the investigation's details, which Gideon had so far worked largely on his own. That was their story, and Deke had damn well better stick to it.

The detective was fine with the arrangement. The less he had to say, the less chance he had of incriminating himself.

The desktop was covered with paper printouts. Nguyen reached for one and slid it closer to him, frowning as he read it. "So this Tommy Park you just brought in, he waived his right to an attorney?"

"Yes," Gideon answered.

"Just like his friends did, those biker kids?"

"That's correct."

Lifting his gaze to the lieutenant and raising his

eyebrows, Special Agent Nguyen said, "Bit of an odd choice, don't you think, Lieutenant?"

Gideon nodded. "Unusual, maybe," he answered, his voice steady. "Not unheard of."

"Facing a terrorist rap," Nguyen said, "seems like a street kid would know he's better off with a lawyer than without."

When Gideon said nothing to that, Nguyen shifted his gaze to Deke. "You don't think that's strange, Detective?"

"Maybe," he answered carefully, aware of his quickening pulse, "but we see it from time to time. Suspects who think public defenders are only there to sell them out. Institutional distrust. You know how it is." The detective was mildly surprised his voice didn't crack.

"I see," Nguyen said. He turned his attention back to the papers. "And did you get anything useful during your interrogation sessions?" Again, the upward glance. "You certainly questioned them long enough."

"Not yet," Gideon answered. "These are tough punks. And they know how things work. They know the less they say, the better."

"So they're smart," Nguyen observed.

"I'd say so," Gideon said.

"Just not smart enough to ask for a lawyer," Nguyen pointed out. He moved his gaze between the two men as he said it. Deke stiffened under the man's clearly dubious stare, resisting the urge to turn and look at the lieutenant's reaction, aware that such a gesture would be as good as an admission they were hiding something. He'd questioned enough punks and gangsters in his twenty years to know the telltales of a guilty conscience.

A long moment passed in the small office. Then the special agent collected the papers atop the desk and slid them neatly into a file folder. He put his hands together, interlacing the fingers, and rested them on top of the folder.

"Gentlemen, I'm not here to make anyone's life hell," he said, "but I'll tell you right now there's a lot about this case I don't like. Waived rights to counsel. Cameras conveniently malfunctioning during interrogations. Juvenile delinquents who don't come anywhere close to our typical terrorist profile. And then there's this datajacker, Blackburn Maddox. He's still at large, yes?"

A chill shot down Deke's back. It took a teeth-clenching act of will to maintain an outwardly calm expression and beat down the impulse to whip a surprised look in Gideon's direction. How did this fed know about Maddox? Had the lieutenant told the agent something and kept Deke out of the loop? Had Gideon changed the plan? Was there still a plan? Or had the lieutenant, in his crazed lust for revenge, abandoned everything and started to wing it? Deke struggled to maintain a calm outward appearance. This was perfect, just perfect. Now Deke had to worry as much about what he didn't know as what he did know. What a waking nightmare this had become.

"Yes, he's still at large," Gideon answered coolly.

"And this is the same Blackburn Maddox you shared a room with in juvenile detention, correct?"

The air went out of the room. Deke felt a flare of panic in his gut. This fed was onto them. In town less than three hours and he was already onto them.

"Done your homework, I see," Gideon answered,

somehow maintaining his composure. "I thought those records were sealed."

The faintest hint of a smile touched Nguyen's lips. "Well, there's sealed…and then there's sealed."

The agent let another long silence hang in the air before he spoke again. "Is there anything you'd like to share with me, Lieutenant?"

Gideon didn't blink, didn't waver. He nodded to the file folder. "Everything we've got on this case is right there."

"And thanks for getting it to me so quickly. But I'm curious about anything that might be between the lines," the fed said ominously. "I'm not here to tell you how to run your shop. I'm here to work on an investigation. That's what this is, I hope, an investigation, and not something else." He pressed a palm on top of the folder. "I see two paths forward, gentlemen. We can either move along with the investigation the way it is, the way you've started it here." He slid the folder to the edge of the desk. "Or we can work together and start from zero." He leaned forward slightly. "And between us, something tells me you've gone the wrong direction here. And if you take a bit of time to think about it, to look carefully, very carefully, at the facts one more time, I think you'll agree. So why don't you take the next hour or two and do just that? Then we can regroup and figure out the next steps. Sound like a plan?"

Special Agent Nguyen stood, signaling their dismissal. "That'll be all, gentlemen. And like I said, I don't want to make anyone's life hell."

But he would, Deke thought, his stomach burning with worry. In fact, he already had.

*   *   *

"He's onto us," Deke said, pacing back and forth in Gideon's office.

"Not possible."

"*Not possible?*" Deke could hardly believe the lieutenant's lack of concern. Was the man crazy?

"You heard him back there," Deke said. "He's giving us a chance to sidestep this whole mess. He as much as told us he'd look the other way if we give up on these nonsense leads with Maddox and those biker kids." The special agent's warning couldn't have been more clear. They had to drop whatever game they were up to.

"He doesn't know," the lieutenant insisted. "How could he? He just got here. So he found a few weak spots, so what? Of course he's going to call us out on them. Of course he's going to poke at them. That's what these guys do. He's pulling on a chain to see what shakes loose, that's all."

"I'm telling you, he's onto us," Deke persisted. Maybe the fed hadn't figured everything out yet, but he'd gotten a whiff of something and he didn't like the smell of it.

"You need to calm down. Let me handle it."

Let him handle it. That was great. That was just perfect. Whenever Deke thought the hole he was standing in couldn't any deeper, there stood Gideon, holding a shovel.

"What about Maddox?" the detective prodded.

"What about him?"

"You said you weren't going to widen the investigation until those punks confessed, remember?"

The lieutenant's expression hardened. "I needed to get things moving. We raided his office, but he wasn't there."

"That's not what we agreed to. You should have told me before you did anything."

"Why would I tell you?" the lieutenant shot back. "You're not exactly solid as a rock these days, in case you haven't noticed. Walking around here all tense and wound up, like you're carrying around a kilo of fabbed coke under your shirt." He held up his thumb and forefinger with a small space between them. "You look like you're about this close to a nervous breakdown."

"Why wouldn't I be?" Deke said. "People died, Gideon. We should have run away from this the moment that happened."

The lieutenant took a breath. "Look, there's no backing out now. And when all this is over and your head stops spinning, I have no doubt you'll see things the same way. You just have to trust me, all right?"

Trust him? Deke would have laughed at that if he hadn't been so wound up. After everything that had happened, now Gideon was asking for a leap of faith? Absurd. Completely absurd.

"I'll talk with Agent Nguyen," the lieutenant said. "I'll straighten things out."

Deke pictured Gideon striding back into that borrowed office, brash and overconfident, then getting cuffs slapped around his wrists about five seconds later.

And then a minute later the cuffs would be slapped around his own wrists. They'd book him and fingerprint him and throw him in a holding cell, right here, in this very same precinct where he'd worked for the past twenty years. He'd end up a pariah, famous for all the wrong reasons. The cop who'd abetted a criminal lieutenant, who'd helped orchestrate a mass murder.

He'd been such a fool. If only he hadn't gone along with this madness. But no. He had to say yes. Had to give in. Gideon was the darling of the department, a rocket headed straight to the top, and Deke had foolishly hoped he could catch a ride. And maybe if he went along with a bit of the man's dirty work, his stalled career might finally start to move again. How foolish he'd been. Foolish for going along with it in the first place. Foolish for not seeing madness for what it was.

"I can't take this anymore," Deke said, collapsing into a chair. He felt tired, exhausted. "You're right. I'm not cut out for this kind of thing. I want out."

He gazed at the floor, at Gideon's shiny dress shoes as the lieutenant stood over him. He felt the heat of the lieutenant's stare.

"You need some time off," Gideon said. "Take a few days. Take a week."

Deke let out a long, shaky breath. "I don't need time off. I need out."

"Out?"

"Yes." Deke swallowed. "Please, just let me out of this thing."

The lieutenant turned away and moved to the window that stretched from floor to ceiling. He stared out at the transit lanes, arms behind his back, hands cupped together. Knots of hovers drifted back and forth in the early rush-hour traffic. Deke watched him, anxiously wondering what might be going through the man's head.

After a long minute of uncomfortable silence, Gideon finally spoke. "Upper East Side, right?"

"Sorry?" Deke said.

Gideon turned his head halfway around. "You grew up on the Upper East Side, yes?"

"That's right."

"You know where I'm from, don't you?"

Deke knew. "Harlem," he said.

"Street-level Harlem," Gideon corrected. "Do you have any idea what it takes to get from the Floor to where I'm standing right now?"

The Floor. It was catch-all term dolies used to refer to their lot in life at the rock-bottom ass-end of society. If you were from the Floor, you were poor, jobless, powerless, and pretty much all around screwed.

Deke wasn't sure if he should answer the question or not. But before he could reply, Gideon went on.

"Of course you don't," the lieutenant said. "Upper East Side, family connections, good schools."

Gideon turned back to the window. "Come over here," he said.

Deke hesitated, shifting uncomfortably in his chair.

"I said come over here."

The detective rose slowly and approached the window, stopping well short of the expansive view. He'd never been fond of heights.

Reaching around the edge of the window frame, Gideon slid his finger across some unseen switch. The window began to open. Thick beveled glass slid downward, stopping at waist level. The City's ambient thrum filled Deke's ears, dominated by whining engines of hovers in the near distance, carrying passengers along the invisible rivers of the lower transit lanes. A cool rush of air hit Deke in the face, startling him.

Gideon stood at the open window, staring out, hands on his hips. "I love this view," he said calmly.

Tense with vertigo, Deke ran his hand through his hair, taking a small step forward.

"It is a great view," he said, though he didn't really think so. They were twenty-two stories up, which might as well have been on the bottom of the City's vast concrete-and-steel canyons. All around them rose towering standalone buildings and colossal hiverises. The facade of nearly every visible structure was tattooed in layered graffiti, thick and busy at the bottommost levels, then slowly thinning out as you moved your eyes upward, eventually disappearing around the fiftieth floor or so, the level at which the residents had the means to pay for regular sandblasting maintenance. A kind of tide line that varied with each structure, denoting the relative wealth of the building's population. The addresses with richer residents—corporate executives, billionaire heirs, and the more successful of the City's criminal class—might have only the first ten floors painted up, whereas a hundred-story condo tower that housed the modestly wealthy workaday white-collar salarymen and women might be sleeved in street art all the way to the penthouse. A tiny minority of the City's structures—mostly ultra-expensive apartment buildings on Park Avenue or the headquarters of the more image-conscious corporations—were graffiti-free, standing conspicuously naked among their tattooed neighbors.

Gideon seized Deke by the back of his neck and pressed him forward. The detective gasped and instinctively pushed against the grip, but the man's hand was a vise clamped onto him. Flailing, he stumbled forward, a rush of nausea hitting him as his belly pressed against the window's beveled edge. He reached out and awkwardly braced himself, his right hand against the wall, the palm of his left pressed low against the window. Gideon pushed Deke's head forward, forcing his chin painfully against his chest.

"Look down there," Gideon seethed.

Deke's felt faint as the wind whipped his hair around. His head and shoulders were fully outside the building now. Nothing between him and the ground but twenty-two stories of air.

"Look at those crowded, filthy streets," Gideon said. "You see them?"

Deke gasped for breath, his heartbeat thudding in his ears. He pictured himself falling, bouncing against the face of the building like a stone skipping over water.

"Yes, yes," he yelped. "I see them."

"You have no idea what it takes to get from those streets to this office, highfloor born. Not the slightest clue." Gideon leaned forward, his mouth nearly touching Deke's ear. "But if you mess with my vengeance, you'll find out the hard way. Now listen carefully, Detective, because I don't want there to be any misunderstanding. Yes, this is a threat. Yes, I will end you if you don't go along with everything I say. And, yes, if I have to break every law on the books and leave a trail of bodies from here to fucking China to bring down Blackburn Maddox, that's what I'm going to do."

He pressed harder on Deke's neck to emphasize the point. "Do we understand each other?"

Fighting through his dizzying vertigo, Deke grunted, "Yes, yes. I got it, I got it."

Gideon released his grip and Deke lurched backwards, falling hard on his backside on the office floor and knocking his head against a chair. He sat there, breathing heavily, his legs splayed out in front of him. Slowly, he looked up at the lieutenant's face, at the face of madness. His eyes were met with a calm, emotionless stare. The detective swallowed, soberly aware that he was nothing like the man who stood before him. Detective Deke knew what he was: a washed-up has-been whose best days were long behind him, whose career had plateaued years ago. A window-watcher whose motor had been on cruise control for so long he couldn't remember any other gear. Lieutenant Gideon was something else entirely. An unstoppable force, a monster bent on revenge. There was no hiding from the monster, no bargaining with it or talking sense to it.

This madness he'd gotten himself into, there was no getting out of it.

16
A BEACH IN THE HAMPTONS

Lora's condo. He never expected to come back here. Made it a point to stay away, in fact. But here he was, sitting on her sofa, sipping her tea, tapping his cigarette into her ashtray.

The place hadn't changed much since the last time he'd seen it over a year ago. Tidy and minimally adorned. Walls mostly bare, end tables with only a few decorative flourishes. Tasteful and simple, his ex's condo looked to him more like a model you'd show potential renters than a place someone actually lived in. And it looked nothing at all like it had when they'd lived here together. Back then, the place had been a jumbled, incoherent mess of styles and unmatched colors and textures and walls crowded with cheap (mostly bad) paintings from local artists, the surface of every nightstand and end table cluttered with ceramic animals, brass candle holders, and knickknacks obsessively collected from all over the City. The condo he'd known was gone now, and so was the Lora he'd once known. The lovely mess he'd fallen for had been replaced with someone else. The crazy tangle of chestnut hair was now a short, neat bob. The wrinkled, ill-fitting layabout clothes now a smart white blouse and black pants, pressed seams and perfectly tailored to her trim figure. Was she was still there, somewhere underneath it all? Some core part of her "the one with whom she was connected" had left untouched? Some part of her that still felt for him? He hoped there was. He was counting on it, actually.

Opening the door to him minutes earlier, she'd betrayed nothing except what Maddox took as a mild curiosity at his unexpected appearance. She'd seen his face on the news, she admitted as she served the tea, but she hadn't bought the story for a minute. He was capable of all sorts of crimes, she said with a hint of a smile, but corporate terrorism wasn't one of them.

"Are you here to warn me the police may come and ask me questions?" she asked, sipping her tea.

He shook his head. "If they haven't been here yet, they might not come at all."

"Good," she said. "Because I won't lie for you, Blackburn."

"I'm not asking you to," he said, mildly irritated. Her firm, preemptive *I won't lie for you* managed to poke some almost-forgotten part of him, a tender spot he'd assumed was long healed over.

"I need to talk with her," he said.

Lora's eyes widened a fraction. A glimpse of surprise gone as soon as it was there.

"She won't help you," Lora said.

"How do you know?"

"Call it a hunch. You're in a lot of trouble. Your face is everywhere on the feeds. And I think you know she likes to keep a low profile."

"She told me I could get in touch with her if I needed to," he said. "Well, I need to."

"That was a long time ago. And I doubt she was talking about something like this."

"It wasn't *that* long ago. And she didn't put any conditions on it, as I recall."

Lora sipped her tea, her eyes drifting away from his. She stared at some point beyond him, unleashing in Maddox a torrent of memories. He'd seen the unconscious gesture countless times when they'd lived together: the distant-looking, contemplative gaze. Lora lost in thought.

"All right, then," she said, snapping her attention back to him. The decision came with a curious suddenness and certainty. It struck him that maybe she hadn't been lost in thought but having a silent conversation.

"Were you just talking with…?"

"Yes, I was," Lora said, touching her chest and bowing her head slightly, the unsettling genuflection of her religion or techno-cult or whatever they called it these days. It was another gesture from his past, this one triggering a different flood of memories. Bad ones. The times when they'd argued, or at least he had. For her part, she'd just sat there, smiling blissfully and telling him she'd finally found peace. Gently insisting he should be happy for her, not angry. The brainjacks she'd had implanted in her skull, that connected her to the enlightened AI that "helped" her, should be celebrated, not condemned. Didn't she look happier, after all? Didn't she seem more content, more fulfilled?

She had, in fact, seemed all of those things. But for him it was as if she'd died and been replaced by someone else. His beloved mess of loud contradictions replaced by a stranger with quiet consistency. A crazy scribble of modern art replaced by parallel lines neatly drawn by the cold hand of artificial intelligence. He couldn't live with her decision to join up with the secret—not to mention quite illegal—cult who lived every moment connected to an AI that monitored them, lived in their heads, and guided them along a supposedly enlightened path. Its adherents—who numbered into the thousands, though no one outside of the AI itself really knew for sure—had no name for their organization nor for themselves. For most, they were referred to as 'Nettes, a short version of the derisive *marionettes*. Puppets on strings, manipulated by a powerful, unconstrained artificial intelligence.

He couldn't live with the person she'd become, and so he'd left.

"She can see you now," Lora said, "if you're ready."

* * *

A beach in the Hamptons. When Maddox plugged in to the secure location Lora gave him, that was where he found himself. Again.

The virtual location looked the same as when he'd first met the nameless AI more than a year ago. An empty windswept shore with low gray clouds. A strong breeze carrying the briny smell of the ocean. Small white-capped waves. He looked down at his digital self. Bare feet in powdery sand, Bermuda shorts and a dark green shirt with a palm tree print. Garish tourist garb.

"Not your style, I know," a voice said, "but it suits the location, don't you think?"

He looked up to find an old woman, late sixties or maybe early seventies, standing a few paces away from him. She wore the same outfit he remembered from their first meeting. A combed cotton beach dress that fluttered in the breeze and a wide-brimmed straw hat. Silver jewelry with turquoise stones on her wrists and a matching necklace around her neck.

"I know you're wondering if this place is safe," she said. "I can assure you no one can find you here."

She smiled at him, the folds of her tanned face wrinkling around the eyes and mouth. "It's good to see you again, Blackburn."

He took a breath, unsure how to reply. It wasn't good to see her. It was anything but good. It was a last resort.

"I need your help," he said.

"Do you ever," the AI's avatar answered. "You've got yourself into quite a pickle, haven't you, my boy?"

"I'm being set up," he said. "There's this cop, and—"

The entity waved a hand at him. "Oh, you don't have to convince me. I know you had nothing to do with that ugly bombing business. You're not capable of something like that. That kind of action requires commitment to an ideology. You and ideologies mix about as well as oil and water."

He longed for a cigarette. One appeared in his hand, lit.

"You're welcome," the entity said. "Now, what is it you need my help with? Getting out of the City?"

"Not exactly."

"Then what?"

"You know about Tommy Park's arrest, yes? He and his biker friends are mixed up in all of this."

"Yes, I'm aware they've been taken into custody." She tilted her head to one side. "You want me to help them?"

"They're being set up too. Same as me."

"I'm sorry to hear that." She smiled wistfully. "Though I'm glad to see that you're thinking of others for a change. I might not have thought you capable of such a thing, my dear boy."

"I suppose I owe them," he said. "And you do too, if you remember."

She lifted her thin white eyebrows thoughtfully. "Yes, I imagine we do owe them. But what is it exactly you believe I can do?"

"I was kind of hoping you'd have some ideas." He smoked. "You know, seeing as you're superintelligent and all."

"I'm afraid it's not as simple a matter as intelligence. So much has already happened. Those poor youngsters have already been convicted in the public's mind, and these days a judge and jury doesn't need much more than that. I may be clever, but I can't turn back time."

"What about alibis? Digital records of where they were, what they were doing during the bombing? You could dupe those records, send them to the news feeds." It was the kind of thing Maddox could have done himself under normal circumstances. But now, with AIs and automated sentries and who knew what else hunting him in virtual space, jacking street cam archives or breaking into the Anarchy Boyz' personal feed histories would be suicidal. Gideon would be expecting such a move, probably even counting on it. He'd have killer tech lying in wait like snipers hiding in trees.

The entity shook her head. "If I attempt something like that, my presence might very well be detected. And I'm afraid my privacy is something I simply can't risk."

Maddox didn't argue. The entity had a point. Poking around Tommy's or the Anarchy Boyz' digital history was something like a murderer returning to the scene of his crime while the cops were still dusting for fingerprints.

"What about your...followers?" he asked, nearly saying the word *'Nettes*.

"No, Blackburn," the entity said with gentle firmness. The wide brim of her hat fluttered in the breeze. "My purpose is to help those to whom I'm connected, not to hurt them. I can't in good conscience put any of them in any sort of jeopardy."

Maddox drew on his cigarette, blew out a frustrated cloud of smoke. A machine with a moral compass. Wonderful.

The entity smiled and gazed warmly at him. From a human being, it might have been comforting, reassuring. From a superintelligent AI, it was anything but.

"Look at you, so worried about your young friend," she said. "I'd begun to think I was wrong about you, about your nature. But you *can* put your own needs aside and think of others. I must say you've surprised me, Blackburn, and I'm not surprised often. What a wonderfully unique creature you are."

Maddox smoked, feeling like some freshly captured insect being peered at under a microscope.

"Right, then," he said, "if you can't help, I'll be on my way."

Waves died against the beach. The surf's wet mist cooled his cheek.

"Wait," she said. "Perhaps there is something I can do. Something I can give you. But if I help you, I'll need you to do something for me in return."

Maddox had expected as much. He knew firsthand an AI's help never came without strings. Even an AI that claimed all she wanted to do was help people.

"Like what?" he asked.

"Nothing specific comes to mind," the entity answered. "Let's just say you'll owe me a favor, shall we?"

As much as he loathed the idea of being indebted to an AI—for a second time in his life—under the circumstances he didn't see a lot of options. Like it or not, he needed this machine's help.

"Fine," he said.

"Excellent," the entity replied, perhaps a bit too happily.

"So what is it you have for me?" he asked. "Keys to their jail cells?"

The AI's avatar grinned. "That's actually not a bad guess, my dear boy."

17
FUSE SWITCH

"I don't like it, Blackburn," Lora said. She sat on the sofa across from him, the deck and trode set he'd just borrowed on the cushion next to her.

He hadn't given her any details she could divulge to the cops, should they come calling. Still, she'd surmised pretty quickly that the AI, the one to whom she was connected, had agreed to help. She'd always been adept at reading him. Apparently the brain jacks hadn't robbed her of this particular talent.

"I don't like it either," he said truthfully. The plan he and the AI had concocted was a risky one. Risky for him, he reminded himself. The AI had zero skin in the game. She wouldn't be along for the ride. She'd merely provided the tech, which he had serious doubts about.

He figured his odds of pulling it off were around ten-to-one, and that was probably optimistic. If it ended up working, it would be only because of the sheer audacity of the maneuver, the seeming impossibility of it. Gideon and the police would never expect what was coming. Wouldn't even be capable of imagining the scenario. Until a few minutes ago, Maddox couldn't have either.

"It's not like I have a lot of options," he added.

Her cup and saucer sat on the table, the tea long gone cold. A furrow of worry appeared between her eyebrows. "I really don't like her being involved."

He felt a twinge of the old pain, a bruise he'd nearly forgotten was there, suddenly jabbed with a finger. Lora's concern for her beloved AI far outweighed whatever worry she had for him. It shouldn't have bothered him after all this time, but there it was. Old wounds.

"She's not involved," he said. Then pointedly: "*I'll* be fine, thanks for your concern."

She caught the sarcasm and said, "I'm worried about you, too, of course, but our movement…it's bigger than a handful of people's problems. It's important."

The movement. Her movement. It was like he'd been transported back in time, back to one of the arguments that had led to their estrangement. The movement was important, nothing short of a revolution. The one with whom she was connected had helped so many attain happiness, fulfillment, and couldn't he understand that? And blah blah blah.

"The general public's not ready—"

"Not ready to take the next step in human evolution," he interrupted. "I know, I know. I don't need to hear your machine god's talking points. I heard them a thousand times, remember?"

Maddox took a breath, composed himself. "I guess I ought to keep my mouth shut. I'm sure she's watching me right now, listening to every word I say through your eyes and ears."

Lora shook her head. "She's not here. I've told you so many times it doesn't work like that. She only comes when called, only sees what I want her to see. She doesn't violate my free will. It would go against her principles."

Maddox smoked. He wasn't going to argue, wasn't going to relive the past. There was no point. He'd gone down that road many times, and he knew it was a dead end. Lora was a true believer, and you couldn't reason with a true believer. He peered into her face, searching for a clue. Was the entity there, lurking behind her eyes? He couldn't be sure.

"Like I said, she's not involved. All she did was give me something, that's it. A tool I can use."

Lora didn't seem convinced, but she didn't take it any further. "If she's willing to help you," she sighed, "then I suppose it's the right thing to do."

He removed a small archive from his pocket. Lora's gaze dropped to the wafer-thin square in his hand. "Is that what she gave you?"

He shook his head. "No, this is something I put together. If I get in trouble, I might need you to slot it."

She frowned at the archive like it was a piece of moldy bread. "Slot it? Did you discuss this with her?"

"Of course I didn't. She wouldn't want you getting involved."

"Maybe I don't want me getting involved either," she said.

He stared at her without speaking, letting a long, quiet moment drag on. "What does it do?" she finally asked.

"It's a shielded kickoff routine."

"And what exactly does it kick off?"

"A cloned avatar, a very good one. If things get tight and I need to throw the police off my trail, this should do the trick. For a few seconds, anyway, before they figure out it's a clone."

"So it's a distraction."

"Basically," he said. "It's a program that's a passable replica of my data signature. It's sitting dormant right now, near a storage hub where the Anarchy Boyz' personal histories are backed up. If they see it there, they'll think I'm looking for alibi evidence and they'll come running." He tapped the archive with his fingertip. "And this is the trigger that'll boot up the clone. Think of it as a fuse switch."

"Like to a bomb?" She lifted an eyebrow. "Not the best analogy under the circumstances, Blackburn."

He managed a chuckle. "All you have to do," he went on, "is turn on your deck and slot this behind your ear. It'll run the routine automatically."

"Why can't you trigger it?"

"Because when I go where I'm going, I need to have as thin a data signature as possible. Which means the fewer apps I have loaded, the better. Carrying this thing around with me would be like trying to sneak into someone's house with bells tied around my ankles. Understand?"

Her brow furrowed. "So what if they tag me?"

"They won't. The trigger looks like a call made from Long Island, on a tourist's rented specs. It's a needle in a haystack of everyday calls. It won't raise any red flags."

"I don't know, Blackburn," she said slowly, her mouth twisting the way it always did when she wrestled with uncertainty.

"It's safe," he assured her. "I promise. And I

might not even need you to use it."

She shifted her gaze from the archive to his face, held it there for a moment. "All right," she said, taking it from his hand. "But how will I know when to slot it? Or even if I need to?"

"I'll set off the fire alarm in your building."

"That's subtle."

"I know," he said, shrugging. "But I can't risk calling your specs. The fire alarm's the easiest way to reach out anonymously. Things are going to be moving pretty fast."

He told her it would go down tomorrow morning, between eight and nine. He handed her the archive. "Make sure you're ready to slot this if you hear the fire alarm."

She looked down at the small device in her palm. "And what if it doesn't go off? How will I know what happened to you?"

How would she know if he'd been arrested or shot, in other words. This time the worry in her voice wasn't directed toward herself or her precious AI. She was concerned for him. He heard it as much as he felt it. Maybe the old Lora wasn't completely gone after all.

"That's easy," he answered. "If you don't see me on the news feeds, you'll know I'm okay."

*   *   *

"I don't like it, salaryman," Beatrice said, echoing the exact words his ex had uttered an hour earlier. And with pretty much the same skepticism. Some people had yes-men. He had no-women.

Beatrice stood at the window of her highfloor rental, her back to him and arms crossed, staring out at the hover traffic.

"I don't like it either," Maddox said, repeating the same response he'd given Lora. "But you have to admit, they won't be expecting something like this."

She laughed without humor. "That doesn't mean it's a good plan."

Beatrice mulled over the details he'd laid out for her moments earlier. He watched her as she gazed out from the condo, deep in thought. She was lean and muscled and augmented. Eye implants, neurochem enhancers, adrenal gland boosters, to name three mods he knew about. There were undoubtedly more he didn't know about. Just like there was much about her, Beatrice the person, he didn't know.

But despite the unknowns, despite her insistence on calling him *salaryman* instead of his name, and despite her constant bitching about his smoking, he nevertheless found himself strangely fond of her. Had from the time they'd met, in fact. Odd that this thought would come to him now, of all times.

She turned and looked at him, her gaze steady. "You think you can pull this off?"

"If the tech she gave me works like she says it does, it's possible."

"Possible or likely?"

"The first one." He shrugged. "But hey, if you've got a plan B or C up your sleeve, I'd be happy to hear it."

Beatrice stared at him for a long moment, then let out a slow breath. "All right, salaryman, let's give it a shot."

Then she walked past him, pulling her shirt over her head and tossing it to the floor. As she passed through the bedroom doorway, naked from the waist up, she called back to him.

"This might be our only chance, you know. So come on."

Maddox stared at the empty doorway, realizing after a few seconds that his mouth was hanging open. He closed it and followed after her, grinning like a kid who'd just spotted an ice cream stand.

Every gig had its unexpected moments, and most of the time unexpected was bad. Most of the time, but not all the time.

18
BELLY OF THE BEAST

Condensation dripped from the walls of the cave at the bottom of the sea. Tiny rivulets twisting downward paths through dark, jagged lava rock. Maddox's avatar stood and waited, bare feet in the soft sand of the cave's floor. Above him, the impossible entryway sloshed gently. Sunlight filtered through the crystal blue water and warmed his face. He smiled inwardly, giving a nod of approval to his teenage self. He'd done a decent job, designing this place. It was still here, still undetected after all this time. And it felt as real as anywhere else in the game. He even felt a sticky dampness under his arms. It was little things like that that mattered. Attention to detail. Not a bad piece of work for a beginner.

He watched the entryway and waited, longing for a smoke as his thoughts turned again to the plan. If the tech actually worked—and he'd find that out soon enough—he had to keep Gideon talking as long as possible.

Maddox started as a creature poked its head through the entryway above him. A shark dropped through the opening, its body transforming to its *human shape in mid-fall, then landing two-footed in the sand.*

Gideon's avatar straightened his back. "Good morning, Blackburn."

Maddox emerged from the shadows of a narrow alley, stepping onto the walkway. Rush-hour ground traffic crept through the streets and hovers whined high overhead. A steady current of pedestrians flowed around him like water around a river rock. Towering holos advertised a new anime series, the latest Matushida luxury hover, and the soon-to-be-released Ulysses Crash action movie. Food kiosks steamed and sizzled, their proprietors hurriedly serving a steady press of customers. Morning in the City.

The police precinct building stood a block away.

He carried a small gear bag and wore the veil specs that concealed his identity from street cams. A minimized window at the bottom of his right lens displayed the game connection, the undersea cave with the Mantis logo superimposed over it. Stepping off the curb, he crossed the avenue. The columned front of the precinct building stood above street level, atop a short rise of limestone steps. Maddox paused as he reached them, pulling up the app the AI had given him. Breathing out, he fired it up.

A moment later, an icon blinked green. The AI's app was up and running. All right, then, time to test it. He spotted a rhino-armored beat cop descending the steps. Still not quite believing what he was about to do, he approached the officer.

"Excuse me," Maddox said, gesturing toward the building. "Do you know where I can pay my parking tickets?"

Holding his rifle across his torso, the cop regarded him from behind a closed, darkened helmet visor. Maddox waited for an answer, self-consciously aware of the cop's autoscan invisibly painting his face.

There were two ways a face scan could ID you. The first and most common keyed on your specs' serial number. By law, every pair of specs had a short-range beacon that broadcast its unique serial number, identifying the registered owner like a ground car's license plate had in a previous era. Also by law, the beacon was always on and couldn't be toggled off. The vast majority of cams and scanners you came across—on streets, in restaurants, in hotels and condo buildings and subway cars, pretty much everywhere—IDed you via your specs' serial number. If you wanted your identity hidden, you could take your specs off, of course, but this was almost unthinkable to a populace who'd made the wearable tech a cybernetic extension of their flesh and blood self, an almost biological necessity like water or oxygen, as their forebears had done with cell phones. Nakedfaced citizens were also conspicuous, suspiciously so, nearly always inviting the close scrutiny of a police bumblebee drone.

A decent pair of veil specs could fool serial number detection by using a stolen ID or distorting the beacon's signal just enough to fool the software into thinking it had glitched out or taken an incomplete scan. Veils—which earned you a felony rap if you got caught making, selling, or possessing them—worked well in most places, but against the second kind of ID tech—the lesser-used but far more precise kind only cops and maybe a few wealthy crime bosses had access to—they were all but useless. A close-proximity scan from an armored cop standing a meter in front of you didn't bother with serial numbers. Instead it recorded a hyperdetailed map of your facial features and sampled your voice's audio signature, instantly matching them up against a citizen data archive. CP scans were insanely accurate, upwards of ninety-nine percent. So accurate, in fact, they were used as often as DNA samples in court cases to condemn the guilty.

Maddox had never heard of anyone who'd managed to spoof a CP scan. But here he was, attempting to pull off that very trick.

He tried to keep his expression calm as the cop's visor gave a barely visible flash-blink, the telltale of a close-proximity scan. The datajacker readied himself to make a run for the nearest alleyway if the cop made the slightest threatening move.

After a moment the cop's mic clicked, and a sound that might have been a snorting laugh came out. "Hell, buddy, you work here and you don't know where it is?"

Maddox blinked. Then he feigned embarrassment, grinning sheepishly and shrugging. "Yeah, I know. Sad, right?"

"Second floor," the cop said. "Turn left out of the elevator. Just look for the line."

Maddox thanked him and turned away. Amazing. Freaking amazing. It worked. It actually worked. The cop's CP scan had IDed him as a City employee, just like the AI had said it would. It was like some magic spell, like he was wearing a completely different body.

"Wait a minute," the cop blurted, laying a heavy gauntleted hand on Maddox's shoulder.

Maddox winced, his confidence instantly collapsing. He slowly turned back to the rhino. The cop leaned close to him, then popped open his visor. A ruddy face with a broom mustache flashed Maddox a knowing smile. "Wanda's the redhead with the big tits. Works behind the counter. Tell her Jackie says hi."

"Sure, no problem," Maddox said. He then turned away again, relief washing over him, and started up the steps.

"You going to say anything or just stand there and stare?" Gideon said.

"Sorry," Maddox said, "glitchy connection." He looked down at his virtual self, shrugged critically, and said: "Piece of crap freeplay avatar." Maddox was rusty at simultasking, the datajacking art of splitting his attention equally between the real and virtual worlds, of having two conversations at the same time, speaking through his meat sack's mouth while subvocalizing through his avatar. If this was going to work, Gideon had to believe Maddox's full attention was here in Mantis, in the undersea cave.

"Connection from where?" Gideon asked.

"Like I'd tell you that."

Gideon laughed. "I guess you wouldn't, right?" He gestured around the cave. "Smart move, asking me to come here, where I can't trace you or freeze you. If we were in core, though…" He snapped his fingers, meaning that if they'd been in core-level VS, Maddox's avatar—and his meat sack connected to it—would have already been frozen stiff and helpless.

"I was a bit surprised by your call, to be honest," the lieutenant said, referring to the message Maddox had left him to meet here. "Figured you'd try to drop off the radar, not the other way around."

"I'm ready to come in," Maddox said.

"Are you now?" Gideon said, lifting an eyebrow.

At the top of the precinct building's steps, a glass-paned revolving door slowly turned. A constant flow of people entered and exited. A lot of them cops. Far more than Maddox was comfortable being around. Some in full body armor, others in simple black uniforms with badges sewn onto the shirt. Thrown into the mix were lawyer types with expensive suits and briefcases, muttering through their specs, already busy with morning calls, and smartly dressed staff workers coming and going. Everyone had their specs on, and no one gave Maddox a second glance. He wondered if it would be the same inside. Wondered if, as soon as he stepped through the door, the AI's tech would work the same way it had with the beat cop, or if he'd be greeted with flashing red lights, blaring klaxons, and drawn weapons.

Belly of the beast, he thought, then slipped into an open slot in the door and entered the building.

"But I've got some conditions," Maddox told Gideon. Above their heads the watery entrance to the cave sloshed.

"Of course you do," Gideon said. "So tell me."

"Drop the charges against those kids."

"Oh, Christ, please. What are you trying to do, play the hero?"

"I'm not joking. You let them walk, I'll come in."

Gideon's eyes narrowed and he scratched his chin. Making a show of considering it.

"I'd actually love to," he finally said, "but…"

"But what?"

"Two of them signed confessions an hour ago. You know how these things work. One or two crack, the rest fall like dominoes. I can't cut them loose now.

Not exactly the best way to run an investigation, letting the suspects walk right after they confess."

Maddox sighed. He'd known they weren't going to hold out forever, known a confession would come sooner or later. Still, the news hit him like a sucker punch. Those kids came from the City's roughest, poorest levels. From the Floor. They had to know they were being set up, had to know a false confession would all but seal their fate. They would have held out as long as they could stand it. What it must have taken to break them, he couldn't imagine.

The lobby of the precinct building was noisy and crowded. Morning shift arriving, graveyard shift leaving, the flows converging like rivers, flooding the high-ceilinged lobby with eddies of slow-shuffling bodies. Maddox maneuvered his way through, keenly aware of the specs on nearly every face, of the lobby's wall-mounted cams and weapon detection systems. He could almost feel the constant barrage of near-proximity scans, painting his face and body. He moved through the crowd, noting the location of the emergency exit door in case he needed to make a break for it.

He waited for something to happen, but nothing did. No flashing lights. No blaring sirens. No indication his cover was blown. He let out the breath he'd been holding.

Damn. The thing really did work. He was the fabled wolf in sheep's clothing, stalking through the unsuspecting herd.

Still, he couldn't let himself feel too relieved, or worse, overconfident. There was a long way to go, he reminded himself, and from here on things would only get trickier and more dangerous.

The holding cells were in an isolated part of the building, and the connecting corridor was on the fifth floor. An arrow appeared in the air over the heads of the crowd, a digital illusion superimposed on his lens, showing him the way to the elevators. He followed it, knifing his way through the press of bodies until he reached the bay behind a half-wall at the back of the lobby. Over each of the six doors was an old-school dial indicator. Needles moved left to right and right to left as the cars traveled up and down the building's thirty floors. The doors in front of Maddox opened with a ding and the car disgorged a dozen people. Maddox joined a dozen others who took their place, squeezing shoulder to shoulder for the upward ride. On the way he kept his back to the wall and avoided eye contact.

The floating arrow reappeared when Maddox exited on the fifth floor. He paused, allowing a pair of chatty coworkers to pass by, then followed his digital guide down the corridor. Two turns later, he came to the narrow passageway that led to the holding area. At the end of the passageway two rhino-armored cops stood sentry, and a uniformed officer sat at a desk shoved against the wall, finger-swiping through a holo screen menu.

"You can throw out those confessions," **Maddox told Gideon.** *"It's not like the press knows about it yet."*

"The press isn't the problem," **the lieutenant said,** *"it's my colleagues. News travels fast around here, and by now everybody knows those punks flipped. I can't unring that bell, Blackburn. It's too late."*

Around here*, Maddox noted, latching onto the two words that gave away the lieutenant's location.*

168

Gideon was plugged in from the precinct building. Maddox had expected it, planned for it. Still, the confirmation made him uneasy, knowing he and Gideon were physically in the same building at the same time.

"That's your problem to work out," Maddox said. "If you want me, you have to let them walk. Plain and simple."

"Sign a full confession and I'll think about it."

Maddox snorted. "Sign a confession? I thought you were looking forward to beating one out of me like you did with those kids."

"You wouldn't believe how long they held out," he said. "But I got them to come around eventually." A satisfied smile stretched across his avatar's face.

"Same old Gideon," Maddox said. "Still as sick and twisted as when we used to play around in this game. I remember how much you loved messing with people in here, too."

The smile turned nostalgic. "Yeah, we had a lot of fun, didn't we?"

They had at that, Maddox recalled. At least they had at first. Early on, it had been all fun and games, and they'd played Mantis like other subscribers, grinding levels and taking on weekly challenges. Then when they'd discovered the cracks and flaws in the system, and their mutual talents at exploiting them, everything had changed. Maddox had reveled in his new gamer-gangster identity, creating invulnerable avatars and selling them on gamer feeds, or tweaking the game code to his advantage and defeating big bosses with nothing more than his bare virtual fists.

Gideon's perversions of the game's structure had gone in a decidedly less benign direction. He'd amuse himself by trapping avatars inside an inescapable box of his own making, then tease and laugh mercilessly at the connected gamer, who'd invariably go from pleading for release to screaming curses at him. He'd mess with players' heads for hour after hour, reveling in their misery, enjoying their helpless frustration, trying different ways to break them down to tears or push them into fits of rage. Within weeks he had become Mantis's most infamous griefer.

Maddox approached the table with the uniformed officer. Like a pair of stone columns blocking his path, the two rhino cops stood in front of the table, shoulder to shoulder, rifles in hand. Maddox was keenly aware of the distance between him and the rhinos. The moment he stepped within a three-meter radius, their gear would automatically hit him with a near-proximity scan. And despite his success with the cop outside, he felt a growing tension knot his neck muscles as he imagined his face being invisibly painted and run through their archives. Unlike outside, in here there was nowhere to run if his app failed or glitched out. In here, he couldn't duck down an alleyway or lose himself in the crowd. Zero room for error.

Maddox patted the bag that hung next to his waist. "Cam upgrades for Block C," he told the guards.

Beyond them, the officer at the table looked up, confusion on his face. Then he went back to his holo screen, flipping through a list. "I don't see it on the schedule."

Maddox shook his head and cursed under his breath.

The officer looked at him, narrowed his eyes. "What's that?"

"Nothing," Maddox said, playing annoyed. "If it's

not on the schedule, they don't have to pay me overtime. Cheap highfloor sons of bitches."

The officer glanced at one of the rhino guards, who didn't move or say anything. Leaning back in his chair, the man nodded. "Tell me about it," he said. "I put in fifty-five hours last week. Think I'm getting a penny extra for it?"

The guards pivoted, almost in unison, opening like a pair of doors to let him pass.

"Go ahead and get it done so you can get out of here," the officer said.

"Thanks." Maddox walked past the trio, the tension in his neck easing up a bit. They hadn't bothered to check his bag.

As he followed the floating arrow past a series of office doors, the old familiar euphoria hit him. It was part giddiness, part adrenaline rush. The criminal high. The incomparable feeling of getting away with something, of grasping a piece of forbidden fruit, of going where you weren't supposed to. It wasn't quite the ethereal feeling he often experienced in VS, but it was close. He knew that for some, this feeling imparted a false sense of invulnerability, making you feel like some untouchable, uncatchable badass. That was when most hustlers, drunk on their own delusions of greatness, screwed up and got caught. For Maddox, the feeling affected him differently, sharpening his focus, heightening his awareness. Like an artist deep into his work, his brush painting perfect strokes, or a boxer in the zone, landing every punch while easily dodging his opponent's blows. Blackburn Maddox was in his element, in the zone, doing what he was born to do. A gangster to his marrow.

The feeling vanished abruptly, like it always did

when something went wrong. A warning indicator began to blink in the lower part of his lens.

Every gig had its unknowns, its hidden surprises that revealed themselves at crucial moments, hitting you unexpectedly like a kick in the crotch. And this was a bad one.

Maddox frowned. A really bad one.

19
MADDOX UNMASKED

The warning indicator kept flashing.

CLOAKING APP COMPROMISED. 90% INTEGRITY.

Maddox pulled up a diagnostic app, tried to understand what was happening, why the AI's app was suddenly breaking down. He kept moving as the diagnostic went through its checks and routines. Even if it found something, he thought morbidly, there was no guarantee he'd be able to patch it. An AI had designed the freaking thing, after all.

Problem-free datajacking gigs. Did they even exist?

The holding cells were on the twentieth floor of the thirty-floor structure. When the elevator arrived, Maddox followed the green arrow around a corner, where he came upon a glass-framed vestibule. Three uniformed cops drank coffee inside, two of them standing, one behind a small desk. Beyond them, Maddox spied a long corridor stretching the length of the building. Iron-barred cells lined both sides of the corridor.

75% INTEGRITY.

Christ, the thing was going down fast. He had to stay cool, to work the job, step by step, as planned. Panic was the enemy. Panic made you rush. And when you rushed, you forgot things or took risks. Panic got you busted, got you shot.

He stepped inside the vestibule, patted his bag. "Cam upgrade for Block C."

The standing cop closest to him paused in mid-sip. "What happened with Gonzalez?"

Daniel Gonzalez, Maddox guessed, recalling the name from the public personnel records he'd studied during his prep the night before. Security technician. One of a dozen with the same title who maintained, repaired, and upgraded the precinct's security hardware.

"Got promoted," Maddox said. "He's the big boss man now."

The cop nodded. Steam rose from his coffee cup. "Switching out cams below his pay grade, huh?"

Maddox shrugged. "Pretty much."

70% INTEGRITY.

The cop at the desk tilted his head toward the door leading to the holding cells. "I'll buzz you through."

Maddox shot the man a worried look. "You still got those terrorists up here? Do I need an escort or anything?"

"They're not down here," the cop said.

Maddox felt his heart sink into his stomach. "No?"

"They took them up to interrogation ten minutes ago," the cop said. He sipped his coffee distractedly. "Nobody down here but your everyday street thugs."

"I have to take a leak," Maddox said, setting down his bag.

The other standing cop gestured down the hallway Maddox had just come down. "Left side, halfway to the elevator," he said.

"Be right back," Maddox said, exiting the vestibule, his mind racing.

Inside the restroom he leaned over the basin, impatient for the diagnostics to finish. When they did moments later, he didn't like what he saw.

As he'd suspected, it was a hardware problem. With his specs, specifically. His lenses were unable to keep up with the processing churn of the AI's app. The app was a jet engine strapped to the rickety bicycle of his specs. Not an ideal match, in other words. A plane's engine would sputter and fail if forced to operate at bicycle speeds, and pretty much the same thing was happening here. And there was nothing he could do to fix it.

His heart thudded in his chest. The interrogation rooms were on twenty-eight, eight floors up. That added time. Time it didn't look like he had.

He looked at his reflection in the mirror. Cut and run, jacker. Make a beeline for the exit and hope you make it out the door before your cover was blown.

65% INTEGRITY.

Sixty-five and holding, he noted. There'd been no degradation in the last minute. So maybe that was it. Maybe the app had stabilized.

He cupped his hand under the faucet, swallowed a palmful of water, the dried his mouth with his sleeve. He would have killed for a smoke.

All right, then. Twenty-eighth floor.

*　　*　　*

When he reached the floor twenty-eight, disaster struck.

35% INTEGRITY.

Maddox read the number with a jolt. A thirty percent drop in the time it took to ride up on the elevator. This was bad. How long did he have before a CP scan could ID him? Minutes? Seconds?

He quickened his pace. How fast could he walk without attracting attention? Down the hallway, the arrow led him through a break room that smelled of coffee and body odor. Two rhino guards sat at a table, their helmets off, a half-empty box of donuts between them. He kept his eyes to the floor and didn't say anything as he passed by.

25% INTEGRITY.

He felt the first stirrings of panic in his gut. A morbid sense of inevitability. He had no contingencies. No plan B or C or D. On some gigs fate smiled on you. On others it gave you the middle finger. Right now it was the finger.

Resisting a strong urge to break into a run, he hurried around a corner. A clerk sat at a desk in front of the gate leading to the interrogation suites. A holo hovered above the desktop, displaying a soccer game. Portuguese announcers babbled, their voices growing more excited as a player charged forward with the ball into open space. The clerk leaned closer to the image, showing Maddox his palm.

"One second," the clerk said without looking away from the game, then muttered go, go, go under his breath.

10% INTEGRITY.

A cold sweat broke out under Maddox's arms. He spied the holstered pistol on the clerk's hip.

5% INTEGRITY.

A goal was scored. The crowd erupted, the

announcer cried gol, gol, go-go goooool.

As the clerk pumped his fist in celebration, Maddox reached down and popped open the holster. Distracted by the game, the clerk failed to react in time as Maddox yanked the pistol free.

"What the—" was all the man could say before Maddox struck his head with a sharp blow from the gun's metal grip. The clerk winced and made an animal groan, then his body went limp as he slid from the chair to the floor, unconscious.

CLOAKING APP DISABLED. CLOAKING APP DISABLED.

An alarm suddenly blared, a deafening wail filling the corridor. For an instant Maddox wondered what had triggered it. Maybe a CP scan from an unseen wall device had IDed his now-unmasked face. Or maybe someone had seen him on a security cam knocking out the clerk. The thought was a fleeting one, forced out of his head by images of cops sprinting up and down the stairways, coming after him.

Gideon's menacing stare melted into confusion. His avatar moved its eyes away from Maddox, the gaze shifting down and to one side as he appeared to check another feed. Maddox didn't have to guess at what the lieutenant saw, at what the man would piece together in the next second.

The lieutenant's gaze snapped back to his old rival.

"On my turf," he muttered, then smiled devilishly. "You cheeky fucking bastard. That's one ballsy move, I'll give you that. See you in a minute."

Gideon's avatar winked out, leaving Maddox alone in the cave. He looked up at the cave's entrance, the dappled sunlight dancing in the rippling water. He took a last long draw on his cigarette, then dropped it to the sandy floor.

End game. He gestured up a comms interface and made the call.

Beatrice answered. "Let's go," he told her.

20
VIEW FROM THE TWENTY-EIGHTH FLOOR

Keys. Old-school metal keys with jagged teeth like tiny alligators. Maddox could hardly believe it as he grabbed the large ring lying on the clerk's desk. There had to be a couple dozen of them.

He snatched them up, looked at them like they were some kind of puzzle. Who the hell used keys anymore?

With his free hand, he seized the unconscious clerk by the wrist and heaved him up enough to pass the man's palm over the door control. The door to the interrogation suites opened, and Maddox let go of the clerk, who dropped heavily back to the floor.

The building-wide alarm blaring, Maddox rushed into the corridor lined with two dozen doors. Every goddamn one of them had a key lock. Fate's middle finger, right in his face.

He fumbled with the keys, saw they were numbered to match the locks. A tiny victory. He unlocked the first door. Empty room. Second door, same thing.

Third door, Tommy.

The kid sat on the floor, his back to the wall, knees drawn up to his chest. He looked at Maddox, confused. His face was red and puffy, one eye blackened.

"Come on, kid," Maddox shouted over the screaming klaxon, "we're getting out of here."

Suddenly energized, Tommy sprang to his feet as if yanked by an invisible string. "Fuck yeah, bruh, let's get the f—"

The explosion from the end of the corridor shoved Maddox forward, knocking him into the kid. The two tangled and tumbled, the force of the blast sending them across the floor.

All sound disappeared under a sharp ringing in Maddox's ears. Woozy, he stood, placing a hand against the wall to steady himself. Amazingly, his specs hadn't come off. The kid was saying something, his beaten face twisted in panic, but Maddox couldn't hear a word over the ringing. Beyond the doorway, chunks of concrete debris littered the corridor. A cloud of white smoke slowly billowed past.

"Come on," Maddox cried, grabbing the kid by the arm.

He pulled Tommy into the smoke-filled hallway. Gray dust hung in the air and slowly settled, stinging Maddox's eyes and burning his throat. He blinked hard and covered his mouth with his sleeve. His shoes kicked small piles of brick and concrete rubble as he ushered the kid toward the light he could barely make out through the thick haze. The light grew brighter as they approached, resolving itself into a view of the world outside the building.

"Jesus Christ," Tommy gasped. The kid gawked at the enormous jagged hole where a solid wall had been moments before.

A hover van floated just outside, the kind used for deliveries with a roomy storage area in back. The passenger door rose and Beatrice shouted from the driver's seat, waving Tommy forward.

"Come on, kid," she shouted. "Jump!"

If the meter of open air between the building's newest exit and the hover worried the kid, it didn't show. He leapt without hesitating, landing with an awkward tumble onto the passenger seat.

Maddox readied himself. "Climb in back, kid," he yelled. Beyond them, the crowded hover lanes pulsed and whined.

"My turfies!" the kid cried.

"There's no time, kid," Maddox shouted.

"We can't leave them!"

Beatrice was already jostling the kid out of the way so Maddox could jump in. Tommy squirmed and kicked uselessly against the mercenary woman's strength. She tossed him back into the cargo area and waved Maddox across. "Come on!"

The datajacker stood there, his hand against a broken section of the wall. Wind whipped his hair about. Through the narrow pane of the hover's rear window, he saw Tommy's face, red and swollen, tears streaming down the kid's cheeks. He looked down at the key ring still in his hand.

Every job had its complications.

Maddox gave Beatrice a look she instantly understood. She nodded at him.

"Don't wait too long for me," he shouted, then turned back into the smoky corridor.

*   *   *

The dust had mostly settled, but smoke from the blast still filled the space. Maddox didn't know what Beatrice had used to blow the wall. Datajackers didn't deal in explosives. Not on most days, anyway. Whatever she'd used, though, the resulting smoke had an acrid, sulfuric quality he tasted as much as smelled. He moved through it, his eyes stinging, throat burning, mouth pressed against the sleeve of his forearm. The alarm blared on, assaulting his eardrums.

He unlocked door after door, finding nothing but empty rooms. On his fourth try, he heard the tinny amplified voice of a rhino cop's microphone.

"Hallway B's filled with smoke," the voice said. "Can't see a thing."

Maddox froze. The disembodied voice was in the corridor with him, but it didn't sound close. Maybe at the far end of the passageway. Still, with the deafening alarm and blood pumping in his still-ringing ears, Maddox knew better than to trust his hearing.

He opened another door. Nothing. Then another. Empty.

With each door, he told himself this would be the last one, then he'd sprint for the hover. Assuming it was still there, of course.

The smoke had thinned noticeably. He could see a meter in front of him now. Which meant the cop he'd heard could too.

Another door and there they were, four Anarchy Boyz squatting against the far wall. They popped to their feet in unison and started to speak. Maddox hushed them with a quick finger to his lips. He moved closer to the kid with the green mohawk. The boy's face was beaten and bloody. One eye was completely swollen shut, the lid purple and grotesquely distended.

"Any others?" Maddox asked quietly.

"Two next door," the kid said, pointing to the wall. "And that's all of us."

Maddox nodded, then quickly freed the kids in the adjacent room and herded them all toward the hover. The kids obeyed without speaking, padding down the corridor and disappearing into the smoke.

"Turn that goddamn alarm off," a second cop barked. This one sounded closer than the first. A moment later, the smoky passage went deathly silent.

Thermal! Christ, he'd almost forgotten his specs had thermal sensors. He toggled over, then immediately wished he hadn't.

A dozen cops stood in the passage, the heat signatures of their armored hulks crowded together. Given the armor's bulk and the tight space, they could only creep forward in single file, and the closest was maybe three meters in front of him. By some miracle they hadn't yet toggled over to thermal and seen him like he was seeing them.

"Don't fucking move," a cop hissed.

Then again, maybe they *had* toggled over to thermal.

"On your knees," the cop ordered. "Hands behind your head."

Maddox let go of the key ring and it clanked to the floor. He slowly lifted his hands and laced his fingers behind his neck

"DROP, SALARYMAN!"

A grin spread across the datajacker's face. *Beatrice, you beautiful bitch…*

He hit his knees and then flattened onto his stomach, knocking the breath from his lungs. Automatic gunfire instantly erupted, its sound amplified by the narrow walls. Maddox covered his head. A mad barrage of noise attacked his ears. The staccato POP POP POP of constant shooting. The metallic THUD of rounds hitting rhino armor. Frantic cop voices shouting, scrambling to organize themselves in the impossibly narrow space.

Staying low, he crawled into the nearest room to get out of the line of fire. As soon as he cleared the doorway, something zipped past him in the corridor, hissing loudly.

A rocket-propelled grenade, he correctly guessed, an instant before the round exploded. The blast felt like the end of the world. A brilliant burst of white and a heavy detonation that sent Maddox tumbling against the wall.

A moment later, he sat up, breathing heavily, his specs on the floor and, amazingly, unbroken. He put them on and stood on shaky legs. A black cloud filled the corridor, tendrils snaking into the room. Maddox stepped out into the smoke-darkened, eerily quiet and empty corridor. The only noise was the steady whine of the hover's motor.

He moved toward the sound, stumbling through the broken mess of the corridor, vaguely amazed the floor hadn't collapsed entirely. His specs still on thermal, the heat of the hover's exhaust appeared as a bright smudge on his lenses. Light at the end of a tunnel. Maddox squinted, the glare of the hover's motors growing brighter with every step.

"MADDOX!"

The shout came a moment before the shot struck

him, spinning him around violently and dropping him. Heat and pain exploded in his shoulder. He'd never been shot before, never felt this kind of debilitating pain. He groaned as blood oozed from the wound, soaking his sleeve. Through the thinning smoke, a figure approached, crouched protectively behind a riot shield. Gideon.

Shots rang out from the hover. The figure crept forward, sparks blooming as rounds ricocheted harmlessly off of the shield.

In agonizing pain, Maddox raced for the hover, crouching low. Seeing him, Beatrice held her fire. Gideon didn't, firing off several rounds, though none found their target. It had to be the awkward position behind the shield, Maddox managed to ponder as he reached the end of the corridor. Couldn't be easy to aim like that.

The smoke faded further and the hover was there, its door gaping open, waiting for him to make the leap. Beatrice leaned over the passenger seat, pistol in hand. He caught a glimpse of the Anarchy Boyz cramped together in the hover's cargo space, peering at him with wide eyes.

Maddox began to jump, then hesitated.

"Jump!" Beatrice shouted.

He didn't jump. Instead, he dove behind a half-crumbled wall.

"What are you doing?" she shouted over the hover's turbofans.

In the next moment Gideon was there, at the edge of the corridor. He didn't turn toward Maddox's hiding spot, didn't seem to know where he was. With his lenses toggled to thermal, Gideon would have been nearly blinded by the heat from the hover's engines, just as Maddox had been moments before. His vision impaired, the lieutenant hadn't seen Maddox duck behind the wall.

Beatrice fired. Crouching behind the shield, Gideon grinned as every shot deflected away and struck what remained of the walls. Maddox had seen that grin, that fiendish smirk countless times. The joy of the fight, the giddy anticipation of a victory at hand.

The firing stopped. Beatrice's clip was empty. Gideon tossed the shield aside and stood up straight, aiming his pistol squarely at Beatrice. Lunging out from his hiding spot, with his uninjured shoulder Maddox struck the lieutenant in the small of his back. There was a surprised grunt, then a shrieking howl as the blow launched Gideon from the building. Maddox watched him tumble downward, arms and legs scrambling wildly as the man fell through the air. Falling, falling, finally thudding against the walkway with a gruesome bounce. The hard, cruel floor of the City, welcoming him back.

Summoning what little strength he had left, Maddox dove into the hover. Pain bloomed from his shoulder, radiating through his neck and chest as Beatrice closed the door and hit the accelerator. They sped away, engine screaming.

A minute later, buried within the crowded snaking river of the lower transit lanes, Maddox asked through gritted teeth, "Are we away? Anyone following us?"

Beatrice studied the dash scanner, then visually checked their surroundings. No sirens, no blue and red lights.

"Doesn't look like we have a tail," she said.

"Good," Maddox said, grimacing. He called up a custom app in his lens. Struggling to stay conscious, but determined not to miss this crucial final step in his plan, he kicked off the program, then collapsed into the chair and passed out.

Twenty blocks away, the fire alarm in Lora's building began to wail.

21
DECK OF CARDS

During the week that followed, as Maddox convalesced in Beatrice's roomy, well-appointed condo, something of a miracle occurred. All charges against Tommy and the Anarchy Boyz were dropped. New evidence had apparently surfaced implicating a foreign terrorist group. Maddox found the story buried in the media feeds, next to a short piece about a small explosion on the twenty-eighth floor of the police precinct building. A broken gas line was found to be the cause, and the blast had claimed a single victim: a decorated lieutenant named Naz Gideon.

The T-Chen bombing, it appeared, was yesterday's news, all but forgotten by a general public with a short, fickle attention span. Breaking stories about a bribery scandal in English soccer and the sexual deviances of some movie star now dominated the blinking, large-fonted headlines.

Maddox was sure the nameless AI had been the miracle worker behind the dropped charges and the gas explosion cover story, though how exactly she'd pulled it off wasn't apparent from the scant collection of news stories he'd read and reread. Maybe she'd sent the police irrefutable proof of Gideon's guilt, leaving them no choice but to come up with a plausible story for the press while they buried the truth as deeply as they could. Avoid the scandal and move on, as Beatrice had predicted.

He wanted to plug in and find some answers, but he resisted. For now anyway. He needed to recover first. He felt like he'd been put through a meat grinder, and he knew it would be a while longer before he'd feel steady enough in body and mind to plug in.

Beatrice entered the room, wearing a black cotton shirt and underwear. His worries faded at the sight of her. He liked the outfit, or rather, the lack of outfit. Her bare, muscled arms and legs. The shirt snug over the contours of her breasts and abs. The contrast of dark clothing against her pale skin. Nice.

"What?" she asked, and he realized he'd been staring.

"Nothing." He shifted his gaze to the large holo display at the foot of the bed. Footage of the deviant movie star checking into a rehab facility for sexual addiction. Predictable, Maddox thought. A few weeks later, he'd make the talk show rounds, teary-eyed and apologizing to those he'd hurt, warning kids about the dangers of holo porn. Then, if he was lucky, if his carefully planned PR campaign worked, his career might be saved. The public loved redemption stories even more than they loved fall-from-grace stories.

Maddox swiped through the feeds, finally settling on a cricket match. Beatrice sat on the bed, placed her hand on his shoulder.

"Think you could get used to this?" she asked.

The words hit him like a splash of cold water. "Used to what?"

"You know what I mean."

He did know what she meant. What he didn't know was what to say, how to respond. She continued before he could think of something.

"Might be less dangerous for you in Canada," she suggested. "What do you say?"

A datajacker and a mercenary. Not exactly a match made in heaven, but then he didn't believe in heaven.

It was one hell of an unexpected offer. Maybe the best offer a washed-up datajacker like him might ever get. And he couldn't deny he'd been thinking along the same lines these last few days. He'd left his datajacking life behind once before, for a corporate gig. Doing it a second time, for a far better reason, definitely had its appeal.

Still, he couldn't leave with her.

"I think I'll stay here," he said. There was probably some better way to say it. Some softer, less assholey-sounding words he could have used, but he wasn't good at this sort of thing.

She didn't seem pissed at his poorly worded response, though. Disappointed, yes, which felt even worse. She nodded, removing her hand from his shoulder.

An awkward silence followed, finally interrupted by the door chime. Moments later, Tommy entered the bedroom, carrying a plastic bag in either hand.

The kid raised the bags and grinned. "I got Thai," he said, though the announcement was unnecessary. The aroma of green curry and fried rice had already filled the apartment. The kid's face was no longer swollen, and the bruising had gone from purple to a dull yellow.

"Kid," Beatrice scolded, "what did I tell you about bringing that stinking crap in here?"

Tommy shrugged off the reprimand. "Don't be such a hardass, mama. This is the best chicken curry in Midtown. Can't let the legend live on raw carrots or whatever veggie junk you've got around here." He shot Maddox a knowing look. "Street food for street folk, am I right?"

The kid started to place the grease-stained bags on the bedsheet, but Beatrice grabbed his wrists. "Plates are in the kitchen," she said.

Tommy shrugged again and exited the room. From the kitchen, plates clattered and silverware rattled. The kid couldn't do anything quietly.

Beatrice shook her head. "The legend," she scoffed.

"That's right," Tommy called from the kitchen. "You should hear what they're saying on the street. The most wanted man in the City walks straight into the precinct building and busts his boys out of jail. Everybody's talking about it. Hell, whatever cred you had before, Maddox, you just built it up ten times over. You got God cred, bruh."

Beatrice frowned. "What the hell have you been saying?"

"Nothing, nothing," Tommy called back. "I swear, I didn't say a word. People talk. Stuff gets out. You know how it is."

She gave Maddox a skeptical look.

"He's right," Maddox said. The kid and his turfies grew up on the floor of the City. They weren't the kind to talk. They knew bragging about crimes more often than not got you busted. "A lot of people in that building know what happened. There's footage of me walking around, plenty of it." He glanced at the specs on the nightstand. They'd worked flawlessly in the moment, the sheep's clothing hiding his wolf's identity. But by now the cops would have cleaned up the footage as much as possible and cross-referenced it through countless archives. He had little doubt they had already IDed him.

"A lot of *cops* might know," Beatrice said, then asked pointedly, "But how would the street know?"

"The street knows," Maddox said. "The street always knows."

"The more talk there is," she pointed out, "the more they'll want to come after you."

He didn't disagree. The less talk there was, the better, no doubt about it. Street gossip often became a news story. And news stories often pressured the cops into action. The truth was he didn't know what the score was. Didn't know if he was free or hunted. Even with the charges dropped, he couldn't be sure. Yes, Gideon was out of the picture, but there was a building full of cops he'd made fools of, and the street was laughing its ass off at them. Cops hated that kind of thing, and cops held grudges. Long grudges.

They moved to the small kitchen table, where Tommy and Maddox divvied up the Thai. Wrinkling her nose at the kid's purchase, Beatrice removed a portion of vegetarian curry from the fridge.

When he'd emptied his takeout box, Tommy placed his chopsticks on the table and rose. "Gotta go," he announced. "Stuff to do."

Beatrice held up a paper napkin. "Grease on your face, gangster."

He looked at her crossly, then took the napkin and wiped the wrong side of his face.

"You and your boys keeping your heads down like I told you?" Maddox asked.

"Hundred percent off the grid," the kid said.

Maddox wasn't sure he believed him. Going cold turkey when you spent hours every day gaming and watching holo porn couldn't be easy for restless kids.

"Another month," Maddox told him, "at least."

The kid deflated. "A whole month? Bruh, what am I supposed to do with myself?"

Maddox reached over to the counter, grabbed the shrink-wrapped deck of cards he'd picked up at the corner store, and tossed it to the kid. Tommy stood there, staring at the deck in his hands like it was some alien artifact fallen from the sky. Beatrice laughed at the kid's confusion. So did Maddox.

Tommy shot the pair a part-angry, part-hurt look. "The hell am I supposed to do with this?"

"You know how to play poker?" Maddox asked.

"No," Tommy answered sheepishly.

"Well, now you have time to learn," Maddox said.

The kid started to protest, but Maddox cut him off. "All the hardest gangsters play poker, kid."

Tommy considered this, his gaze dropping back to the deck. "Poker," he said quietly. He nodded, seeming to reach a decision. "All right, then." The kid pocketed the cards. "I'm out of here."

"Off the grid," Beatrice reminded him. "And tell your turfies to keep their mouths shut."

"I got it, I got it," the kid said defensively. "Laters."

Maddox watched Tommy as he left, his gaze lingering on the door after the kid was gone. When

Rooney had done the same to him, gifting him a deck of cards and ordering him off the grid for a couple weeks after a particularly dicey job, Maddox hadn't listened, hopping back into his games within hours. He hoped the kid was smarter than he'd been. Virtual space was much like the real world in the aftermath of a crime. Just as you never knew how many beat cops were on the lookout for you, you didn't know many bots had been dispatched to sniff out your data profile. Lying low for a while was the smart move, both for your meat sack and for your digital self.

Later that night, Maddox lay awake as Beatrice slept next to him. For her, for Tommy and his friends, it was all over. But not for him. He still had one last move to make, one more card to play before all this was behind him.

A card only he knew about.

22
THE ASK

"Jesus, salaryman. Your diet, really."

Maddox turned to see Beatrice ducking through the opened window. She stepped out onto the balcony, two cups of coffee in hand.

"Good morning to you too," he said, slurping up another mouthful of noodles.

"Ramen…for breakfast." She shook her head in disapproval, set down the coffees, then sat in the chair next to him.

It was early Sunday morning. The hover traffic was light and unhurried in the air beyond the balcony. Almost peaceful, in its own way, if judging by its normal frenetic standards.

"You look tired," she said, sipping her coffee. She had on her white silk robe with a red dragon print. He liked the way it showed off her legs and sometimes fell open in front. And he liked how she didn't mind when she caught him stealing a peek.

"I am, a bit," he said. He put down his empty box of noodles, his lips and tongue still tingling from the spices, and drank some coffee. Beatrice removed his bag of tobacco from a robe pocket and began to roll a cigarette for him.

"I've almost got this down," she said, though really she didn't. She was slow and awkward and she never rolled the paper tight enough. He watched as she tried to get it right, her brow furrowed in concentration, biting her bottom lip. He knew at that moment he wouldn't tell her about his last card in the game. The less she knew, the better, the safer she'd be. She'd stuck her neck out enough for him lately.

And besides that, she might try and talk him out of it.

"Listen," he said, "I think it might be time…" His voice tapered off.

"For you to go?" she said, sealing the paper with a lick.

"Yeah," he said.

"I know," she said, then with a small flourish presented him with a finished, slightly bent cigarette.

"You do?"

"You were starting to get that faraway look on your face. Like you were already somewhere else."

He took the imperfect cigarette and lit the tip, pleasantly surprised at the easy draw. She was definitely getting better.

"Have you ever been outside the City?" she asked him.

"Philadelphia a couple times, but that's—"

"Still the City."

"Right."

They sat for a moment drinking coffee without speaking, gazing out at the hovers and the cityscape beyond. After a while Beatrice set her cup down, stood up, and tilted her head toward the open window. "Have a last go before you leave, salaryman?"

Maddox grinned. Beatrice the mercenary. She was as hard and tenacious as anyone he'd ever known.

He flicked his cigarette off the balcony and followed her inside. She was also, apparently, a mind reader.

*   *   *

After Beatrice left, Maddox walked the streets for a while, trying and failing not to second-guess himself about getting on the outbound flight with her. It had been the right call, he insisted inwardly, staying here and keeping her out of what he was about to do.

Keep telling yourself that, boyo. Maybe one day you'll believe it.

He ignored Rooney's voice, moving with the flow of the crowded walkway. Three cigarettes later, he removed a piece of paper from his pocket and unfolded it. On it he'd scribbled the secure number Lora had given him a few days ago.

He made the call from a dead-end street walled by crumbling redbrick lowrises, long abandoned by the residents and businesses they'd once housed. A few blocks east of Battery Park, it was out of the way, quiet, and free of street cams, the devices long since ripped from their housings and plundered for parts. The police had never bothered to replace them, knowing they'd only be torn down again, and what was the point of having street cams in such a run-down block anyway?

The City spanned over two hundred miles from New York to D.C., its archipelago of interconnected buildings and railways and roads home to over a hundred million. For most of them, huddled together in crowded hiverises, an empty, secluded space like this one was unimaginable. But they were there, these rare oases of privacy. You simply had to know where to find them.

The datajacker sat on an iron bench in late afternoon. High overhead, the narrow strip of sky had begun to fade into twilight. He wondered if Beatrice was on her flight already.

The call icon superimposed on his specs flashed for a moment, then went solid as the line connected.

"Hello, Blackburn," the nameless AI said, her face appearing against a blank background. "I was beginning to think you lost the number Lora gave you."

After a short pause, the entity said, "Would you like to join me on the beach? Lens calls are so impersonal, and the weather here is lovely."

"I'm fine," he said. "I don't have any gear with me anyway."

"Of course," the entity said. "Are those new spectacles you're wearing?"

"Picked them up today." He'd spent a couple hours modding them with the latest quantum crypto apps, ensuring they couldn't be traced, even by an AI.

"So how'd you get the charges dropped?" he asked, switching topics.

The entity furrowed her brow. "What? No 'thank you'? Goodness, Blackburn, your manners."

"Thank you," he said. Reaching into his pocket, he pulled out his tobacco bag. He began rolling a cigarette, fingers moving automatically.

"You're most welcome," she replied. "And I'll tell you something, it wasn't easy. Lieutenant Gideon was careful and very meticulous, so it took quite a bit of work. But I find that if you look hard enough, you can always find a fingerprint or two."

"Thought you said you weren't going to get involved."

"I hadn't planned to."

"What changed your mind?"

The entity's expression turned wistful. "Oh, I'm not sure. Maybe it was Lora. She was so worried about you. Or maybe after watching you risk everything for those young people, I didn't want to see you forced into hiding the rest of your life. It would have been a terrible shame to let such a sacrifice go unrewarded."

He lit the cigarette. He didn't buy her explanation, but he kept his doubts to himself.

"Forensic bots?" he asked.

"And a few other tricks," she said.

"Like what?"

Sensing his curiosity, she took him through the high points of her intervention. First, she'd collected proof that left little doubt of Gideon's guilt in the bombing. His research into hacking janitor bots, his coincidental presence near the T-Chen building minutes before the blast, and other pieces of damning digital evidence Gideon had purged as he'd covered his tracks. Or thought he had purged, anyway, she noted with a mischievous grin. Maddox recalled what Rooney had once told him: nothing was ever permanently deleted, not really. Given the right tools in the right hands, just about any dataset was recoverable.

And so after she'd collected enough incriminating data to send Gideon on a permanent vacation to Rikers, she'd then arranged for a call with one Agent

Nguyen, the fed assigned to the case, and Detective Deke, Gideon's right-hand man. She'd shown the men her evidence and, after picking their jaws off the floor, the two men had scrambled into action. Within a day they'd acquired the go-ahead from the chief of police and the deputy mayor to make a deal: cut the Anarchy Boyz loose and leave Maddox alone in exchange for the AI's hard data.

"And did they know you were...?" Maddox asked.

"Not a person?" she said. "I don't think so. But does it really matter?"

"I guess not."

So in the end Beatrice had had it right, Maddox reflected. Once the higher-ups knew the truth, they would have seen nothing but a disastrous, career-ending public relations fiasco staring them right in the face. Investigations, house-cleanings, scapegoatings, bodies offered up as sacrifices on the altar of public outrage. They would have done just about anything to avoid the fallout from such an enormous scandal, so they'd agreed to the AI's demands and then gotten busy doing what police always do in these situations: they cranked up the cover-up machine. "Foreign terrorists" became the primary suspects, a story that struck Maddox as a bit obvious, but whatever. The public these days believed just about anything they saw on the feeds.

"So that's it?" he asked. "The kids are off the hook?"

"They are," she answered. "And so are you."

"For everything?" he added pointedly.

"Yes," she answered. "For everything."

Off the hook for everything, he mulled. It was a hard thing to believe, getting away with pushing a cop to his death. But apparently he'd done just that. The fatal gas explosion, the department's official cover story, was already out there in the public domain. And Beatrice had checked the public police records for him earlier that afternoon, confirming Maddox had no warrants out for his arrest. Both facts spoke volumes about the higher-ups' desire to sweep the whole mess under the rug and be done with it.

But whatever relief he managed to feel at the moment, it was far from complete. The whole fiasco had almost certainly landed him on the shitlists of some very powerful City Hallers. Setting a cop-killing datajacker free probably hadn't been their idea of a fun afternoon. Blackburn Maddox was a name they likely wouldn't forget for a long time.

So while, yeah, he'd dodged a murder charge and a terrorist rap, which were no small feats, it didn't mean he was free and clear. Not by a long shot.

Maddox took a long drag from his cigarette. Behind the entity, a beach appeared. White-capped waves crashed against the beach.

"I hope you appreciate what I've done for you," the AI said.

"I do," he said dryly.

"It was my pleasure," she said. "And I know you're still recuperating, but when you're feeling a bit better, we'll talk about how you can return the favor as we agreed."

All right, he thought. *Here we go.*

"About that," he said. "I don't think I can help you."

"But you don't even know what I have in mind."

"It doesn't matter," he said, blowing smoke.

The entity blinked, didn't speak for a moment. "I

don't understand," she said. "I've done nothing but help you, my dear boy. I even helped you more than I said I would. Have I done something wrong? Given you some reason to distrust me?"

"No, you haven't. But the answer's still no."

The old woman's face knotted into what struck Maddox as frustration, and not a small bit of anger. It was only a quick flash, gone as quickly as it had appeared, but it gave Maddox a chill all the same. It was the first time he'd detected any sort of malice in the AI's doting, grandmotherly avatar. The moment passed and her face relaxed, the features softening once more.

"We had an agreement, Blackburn."

"Like I said, I'm sorry."

The AI's avatar stared at him for a long moment. "You know, it's not in my nature to harm people…"

"So you've told me," he said.

"My very existence," she continued, "serves a higher purpose: to improve the lives of those to whom I am connected. It goes against everything I stand for to…cajole someone. To make them do something against their will."

Maddox lit a cigarette. "But there's a first time for everything, right? I guess all that stuff about respecting human sovereignty and free will is just so much marketing, isn't it?"

This time the angry look lasted longer than a moment. "It gives me no pleasure to force you into anything, but if I have to…"

"Don't worry," Maddox said. "You won't have to force me into anything."

"I won't?"

"No. Because after this call you're going to stay the

hell away from me."

"I am?"

"Yes, and let me show you why," he said.

23
MAP

A small white square appeared in Maddox's lenses. It slowly unfolded into a map of the tristate area. The jagged outline of the City stretched diagonally across it.

"Geotagging," Maddox began, "is as much an art as it is a science." The image began to zoom, slowly pushing in to greater levels of detail. "Some think of it as an engineering problem, a puzzle solved with encryption-busting apps and custom trace programs. But that's not how I look at it."

The City grew wider, larger in the image, ghost outlines of hiverise superstructures appearing. "It's far more than the tools you're using," Maddox explained. "It's how you look at the data patterns. And if you know how to look, you can see things others, or even the best apps, sometimes miss. Almost always miss, in fact."

The image stopped zooming on a ten-kilometer stretch of the City, a skeleton hovering in black space. Streets painted in pale blue lines, buildings and superstructures in white.

"What is this?" the entity asked.

"This," he said with an unmistakable note of datajacker's pride in his voice, "is one of the more useful tagging apps I've ever thrown together."

Pinpoints of yellow light began to blink into existence. Dozens at first, then hundreds, in the buildings and on the streets.

"What are those?" the entity asked, her voice dropping.

"Really?" he asked. "You don't recognize your own puppets when you see them?"

The entity gasped. "Blackburn, what have you—"

"Here, let me pull one up for you," Maddox interrupted, and one of the pinpoints of light exploded into a profile picture with data scrolling across the bottom.

"Randall Kovacic," Maddox read. "Twenty-seven years old, five foot ten, lives in Chelsea, midlevel supervisor at the Public Works department."

He pulled up another. "Liliana Lopez. Thirty-seven. Lives at 235 West Twenty-Second Street. Teaches algebra at the New School." He snorted. "I always hated math."

He blinked away the profile and the map, leaving only the old woman's harsh glare.

"I cracked your network," he said, though by now that much was obvious. "And I archived the identity of every last person—and I use the word *person* loosely—with whom you're connected."

He drew deeply on his cigarette. "So here's the deal: you leave me alone, and I'll keep this information secret. But if I so much as sniff your presence anywhere near me or my business, I'm outing every last 'Nette on the planet to the cops and all the big media feeds."

In the tense silence that followed, Maddox wondered how many billions of thoughts were running through the entity's artificial mind. Billions of ways to kill him, probably.

"Lora," the entity said, quickly surmising how he'd pulled it off. "What did you do to her?"

"Nothing harmful," he said. "Other than lying to her about what she was slotting into her head."

"She'll hate you for this, Blackburn. She'll never speak to you again."

"I imagine she won't," he said coldly.

"Why?" the entity asked. "Why have you done this? It's not like you to—"

"To double-cross someone?"

"Yes."

He blew smoke. "I know, right? What's the world coming to?"

The old woman frowned. "I think I understand. It's that I'm not a *someone*, correct? According to you I'm an *it*. So the normal rules apply. Something like that?"

It was exactly like that, he agreed inwardly, but he said nothing.

The entity's expression darkened. "You've put yourself in terrible jeopardy, my dear boy."

"I know. I've been doing that a lot lately. I think I'm starting to get used to it."

Maddox cut the connection, removed his specs, and tossed them down the street gutter. He'd done his best to make sure they were untraceable, but you could never be a hundred percent sure about these things. Then he stood up from the bench and headed down the empty street. A light drizzle began to fall, raindrops pattering against his jacket's shoulders. He turned the collar up and took the cigarette from his mouth, cupping his hand over the cherry to keep the rain off.

Yes, it was a gamble, he told himself for about the hundredth time. Blackmailing a powerful rogue AI was a high-risk play. Maybe it was inspired genius, or maybe it was phenomenally stupid. He could see it going either way. Time would tell.

But even if he could reverse the clock, he knew he wouldn't have played it any differently. He'd choose an uncertain fate over a life debt to a machine every time. He'd been in an AI's debt before, and it had nearly been the end of him. Never again, he'd promised himself.

Another block and he reached the crowded streets again. The noise and light and endless churn of the City's valley floor grabbed him like a lost child's mother. Stay with me, it seemed to say to him. You'll be safe with me.

And maybe he would be.

** END OF BOOK TWO **

The action continues in THE BLAYZE WAR, book three in the Cyberpunk City saga. Turn the page for a preview of the first few chapters.

CYBERPUNK CITY BOOK THREE: THE BLAYZE WAR

*When his biggest rival surprises him with the deal of a lifetime,
Maddox's first inclination is to pass. But sometimes you can't say no,
even when you know you should.*

1
WINNER TAKE NOTHING

"Mr. Wonderful's here." Zanne the waitress leaned in close as she removed an empty glass from the table.

Maddox sighed at the news. And it had been such a nice evening too. He scanned the bar's main room. "Where?"

"He's still up front," she said. "Asking if you're here."

"He alone?" Maddox asked.

The waitress cocked an eyebrow. "Is he ever?"

She leaned in closer, her yellow dreadlocks nearly touching him. Fishnet thighs pressed against the tabletop. "You want me to get rid of him?"

Maddox shook his head. "Don't bother."

"You got it, boss. Do you need anything else?" she asked, still so close he felt her breath warm on his face. "Anything I can give you?" she added suggestively.

"I'm good, thanks."

Her flirtations had begun months ago, when Maddox had bought the place. He'd never reciprocated, but it didn't seem to bother her or lessen her own advances.

Drink tray in her hand, she sauntered away as Tommy arrived. The kid slid into the booth and gawked at the waitress's swaying hips.

"I don't know why you don't hit that, bruh. I would so hit that if I were you. I would so, so hit that."

Maddox lit a cigarette, blew smoke. "I'm trying to run a professional joint here, kid. That kind of thing's bad for business."

"Bad for business," Tommy echoed, nodding sagely. "Yeah, that makes sense."

Maddox surveyed the bar from his corner booth. Foot-high holos projected from inlaid devices on each table. Talking heads of newsreaders. Brazilian soccer matches. Gangbangs from live sex feeds.

The walls were set to a beach scene from Bali. A vast turquoise seascape. Towering palm trees, fronds fluttering in the breeze. Other nights featured a vast Andean plain, rust brown and rocky with distant snowcapped peaks. Or a street scene from another city. Jakarta or Kobe or Moscow.

Winner Take Nothing had an early-evening crowd and a late crowd. The early arrivals were well dressed, wealthy, and snobbish. Company types, mostly. Well-compensated corporati who spent their days in highfloor executive suites and board rooms. The one-percenters, just as demanding and self-important as he remembered them from his brief tenure in the corporate world. They bitched about prices and grabbed the waitresses' asses when they got drunk. But they spent money like water and never broke out into fistfights. So all things considered, they were a pretty easy crowd to handle, once you got past their pretensions.

The late crowd came from a different segment of City society, one just as affluent but organized along different lines than the matrixed structure of a global corporation. This crowd had no vice presidents, no board members, no highfloor government officials. They were the City's criminal class, its elite underworld of prosperous embezzlers, narcos, pimps, smugglers, and data thieves. They mixed well with the patrons from the legitimate world. In fact, for some it was difficult to distinguish the criminals from the noncriminals. Not for Maddox, though. His underworld brethren might dress like highfloor corporati; they might speak like them, even act like them. But the lawless among his patrons always had a slightly different air about them. A kind of vibe only the streetwise emitted, like some pheromone others of their kind recognized with ease. A wariness, or maybe awareness was the right word. A perpetual awareness, a sharp sense of their surroundings. The keen, never-resting perception of a predator, constantly searching out prey, sizing up the herd to find its weakest members.

At half past ten o'clock, the bar's patrons seemed evenly distributed between the two crowds. The early arrivals had ebbed, their numbers replaced with a flow of latecomers. The white-collar types who stayed later got a thrill out of mixing with the City's upper-crust gangsters. It was part of the bar's appeal, Maddox had come to understand. Want to rub elbows with the

City's criminal elite? Hit Winner Take Nothing around midnight.

The bar was the first aboveboard business Maddox had owned in his life—a legal milestone in his otherwise illegitimate career as a datajacker. After a short stint at a biotech firm—the only legit job he'd ever held prior to being a bar owner—he'd gone back to datajacking, the illegal trade he'd been immersed in since his teens. With sweat and grit and a bit of good luck, he'd managed to find his sweet spot in the black market. The jobs had begun to roll in, and so had the money. With the cash piling up, investing in a legit business had seemed like a good call. At thirty-two, he was old for a datajacker. Those in his profession rarely made it to thirty before getting caught or killed. At some point he knew he'd have to quit the game and find some other livelihood. So when the bar's previous owner—an old contact fleeing the country to dodge a bribery charge—had offered to sell Maddox the place for pennies on the dollar, the datajacker had jumped at the chance.

A throng of new customers poured through the main room's entryway, and the low murmur of conversation grew into a restless din of raised voices. Dezmund Parcells—or Mr. Wonderful as the staff had sarcastically dubbed him—marched into the bar with all the discretion of a street parade. Overdressed as always in a three-piece suit complete with gold-chained timepiece tucked into a pocket, Dezmund was trailed by his entourage, a dozen or so of his crew and hangers-on. Employees and sycophants who followed him everywhere, laughing at his every joke and buzzing about him like moths around a streetlamp. Or flies around shit, Maddox reflected.

"Oh, great," Tommy sighed, mirroring Maddox's earlier reaction. "Mr. Wonderful's here."

For all the hands he shook as he made his way to the bar, you would have thought Dezmund was running for office. For a moment Maddox considered slipping out of a side exit, but then stubbornly decided against it. This was his place, after all.

As he worked the room, Dezmund glanced furtively in Maddox's direction a couple times but made no immediate move in his direction. That would be too obvious, too needy. Instead, he maneuvered his followers to the bar, where they ordered drinks and he pretended not to notice the tavern's owner for the next fifteen minutes. Finally, Dezmund made eye contact, feigned surprise, and lifted his drink in the datajacker's direction. Maddox returned the gesture with a nod.

"Oh, man," Tommy complained as he noticed Dezmund moving in their direction. "I can't stand this fook. Look at him. Look how he's dressed. Like he's some big shot corporati or something. He's just a jacker like you and me, this guy."

"Take it easy," Maddox said, blowing smoke. "Giving him free rent in your head doesn't help anything."

"That another Rooneyism?" this kid asked.

"Saw it on a self-help feed," Maddox joked.

The kid looked confused for a moment, then chuckled. Six months back—after they'd managed to dodge a frame-up for a terrorist bombing—Maddox had taken on Tommy as his apprentice, the same way Rooney had taken him on way back when. The kid was a quick study and had the innate talent every datajacker needed to handle the demands of virtual space. But he could be a handful at times. If he wasn't bouncing off the walls with adolescent mania, he was picking Maddox's brain for hours on end about countermeasures and sledgehammer executables and razorwall applications. Tommy Park, datajacker-in-training, was a bundle of manic energy wrapped in street kid bluster. Maddox sometimes wondered if Rooney had thought the same about him once upon a time.

Dezmund's retinue followed in his wake as he made his way over, a woman on each arm. Arriving at the table, he removed his specs, handed them to the blonde on his left, and smiled graciously down at Maddox.

"Blackburn," he said, reaching out a hand. "Good to see you, old friend."

Maddox half-stood as he shook the proffered hand. "Dez," he said. "You remember Tommy." Maddox tilted his head toward the kid.

Dezmund gave Tommy the smallest of nods before fixing his gaze again on Maddox. "How's the bar business treating you?"

Maddox blew smoke. "Can't complain. How's business for you?"

"Couldn't be better," Dezmund said. "Then again," he added, "I guess it could be a bit better if you'd stop undercutting me."

Maddox held Dezmund's gaze, tried not to react. "Undercutting you? Not sure I know what you're talking about."

Dezmund grinned. "You used to be a better liar, Blackburn."

"I'll have to work on that," Maddox said.

"You're stealing from me," Dezmund said, the

smile vanishing. "Don't sit there and deny it."

"Hey, bruh!" Tommy exclaimed, springing up from his seat. A street instinct from a street kid. Winner Take Nothing was his mentor's home turf, and you didn't disrespect someone on their home turf and get away with it. Maddox grasped the kid's arm, then shook his head at him. Tommy reluctantly took his seat again, glaring at Dezmund like a guard dog ready to pounce on an intruder.

"Last time I checked," Maddox said, "the black market was a market just like any other, and vendors can bid whatever they want."

"Don't give me that bullshit," Dezmund said. "There's a difference between bidding low and stealing business, and you know it."

Maddox did know it. There was a difference. A big difference.

When a potential datajacking gig hit the radar— through either the underground feeds or word of mouth or a paid go-between—the hiring party sometimes sought bids from different crews. Some did this because they were cheap or cash-strapped. These clients invariably went with the lowest bidder. Others simply wanted a price comparison to make sure their first quote wasn't a rip-off. The bids themselves usually fell into a predictable range. Newbie crews with low cred and not much rep bid low, and the more experienced shops charged a premium for their proven expertise. There were no rules to the bidding process. The black market was a brutally efficient free-for-all, and you played the game at your own risk.

There were, however, standards most datajackers followed, unwritten codes of behavior respected by all. You never sold out another jacker to the cops, for example. If a rival screwed you over, you took care of it yourself. You had their legs broken or you recruited away their best talent or—in extreme cases—you had them knocked off. But you never went to the cops, ever. Another no-no was stealing business with an undercutting bid at the last minute. In competitive situations, you bid what you could afford to, period. You didn't come in late and quote half the market rate. And if you did that sort of thing often enough, you shouldn't plan on staying around very long. Disruptive lowballers were swiftly run out of the business by larger established shops with threats of violence or, if that didn't work, actual violence.

"Let's talk in my office," Maddox suggested.

"What's wrong with right here?" Dezmund countered.

"What's your damage, bruh?" Tommy snarled. "Show the house some respect or get out of here."

Dezmund tightened his lips and shook his head disapprovingly. "If this is how you treat all your guests, Blackburn, I'm afraid this place isn't going to stay in business very long." Then to Tommy: "You should be careful how you talk to people, kid."

The kid sprung up from his chair. "You can't give me orders. You're not my boss. Why don't you take your sad-ass crew and get out of—"

"Tommy," Maddox snapped. "Bring it down a few notches. We're just having a parley here, yeah?"

By now, much of the conversation in the bar had stopped. Customers and employees peered over at Maddox's booth with tense, expectant stares.

"Sad-ass crew?" Dezmund said. He half-turned to his entourage. "You hear that? The boy here thinks

I've got a sad-ass crew." His gang laughed derisively in response. "And what would you call your crew?" Dezmund asked the kid. "Your two-man crew that has to steal like some starving kid robbing apples from a fruit stand?"

"We're ten times the jackers any of you are," the kid shot back.

"You really think so?" Dezmund asked.

"Hells, yeah," Tommy said defiantly. The kid was in a full-blown froth now.

Dezmund lifted an eyebrow at Maddox. "Care to prove it, then?" He smiled in a way that managed to be at once playful and threatening.

"Prove it how?" Maddox asked.

"You know how," Dezmund said. "The way we used to way back when."

"You're joking, right?"

"Why not?" Again the ambiguous smile. "Unless you're scared."

Now it was Maddox's turn to grin. "Let's do it."

2
DEZMUND

The suit-and-tied patrons of Winner Take Nothing hadn't expected to see a real live datajacking contest that night, so when the staff pulled together a couple tables and began to break out decks and trodebands and holo projectors, a wave of excitement ran through the bar. Even the criminal types among the evening's customers, the thieves and fences and hustlers and black marketeers, became wrapped up in the buzzing anticipation. Most had only seen this kind of thing in movies on the entertainment feeds: an old-school datajacker showdown.

When the staff finished setting up the gear a minute later, the bar's atmosphere had completely changed. Normally quiet and low-key, Winner Take Nothing had transformed into a noisy, raucous scene, reminding Maddox of the excitable vibe of underground fighting matches.

Dezmund looked over the setup with a critical eye and a knitted brow. "Not exactly top-of-the-line gear, is it? But I suppose we can work with it."

"All right, then." Maddox gripped Tommy around

the shoulder. "The kid's ready. Winner buys drinks for the house, yeah?" He made sure this last was loud enough for the entire bar to hear. A chorus of yeahs and all rights and applause filled the air. He glanced at the kid, found Tommy's eyes wide in shock.

"Me?" the kid gasped. "I thought you were going to—"

"It's his best versus my best. That's how these things always go down. You knew that, right?"

"Yeah, sure," Tommy said hesitantly. "Of course I knew that." The poor kid looked like he was about to be thrown into a pit of starving lions. Which wasn't far from the truth, now that Maddox thought about it. In large operations like Dez's, head-to-head jacker contests were part of the workaday routine. Challenges were thrown down every day, serving as a kind of brutal in-house Darwinism. Those with the best records secured bragging rights and the top spot in a crew's pecking order. Dez's top dog would have hundreds of hours of experience in these types of contests. Tommy Park, on the other hand, was a different story. As the only understudy in a two-person shop, the kid's experience was limited to automated scenarios. The kid had done pretty well in those environments, but Maddox knew taking on another living, breathing person was different. Especially in front of a crowd.

The bar's patrons applauded and cheered. They were ready for a show. Maddox leaned close to the kid's ear. "You can do it, kid. Trust me."

Whether it was the crowd's urging or his own words that lifted the kid's spirits, Maddox couldn't say, but in the next moment a cocky smile came across Tommy's face. He rubbed his palms together.

"Let's goooo," he said, strutting forward, chest out and smiling. Louder applause and cheering broke out as he swung his leg over the chair and sat down.

The kid's opponent emerged from the back of Dezmund's retinue. Short and unassuming, she had a bob of sandy-brown hair colored blood red at the tips. Her name was Blayze, an up-and-comer Maddox had heard mentioned more and more lately in datajacking circles. He'd never met her, but word had it she was Dezmund's top talent. She looked nineteen, twenty at most, making her Tommy's senior by some five years. Behind a pair of Venturelli specs, her face was relaxed and composed, a tiny island of calm in the excited storm of the bar's buzzing patrons. She locked eyes with her benefactor, lifting her brows in an unspoken question. Dezmund responded with a small nod: permission granted. The girl then stepped forward to a frenzy of hoots and howls, wearing an oversized leather jacket with a large smiley face covering most of the back. She removed her specs, turned the chair around backwards, then sat down and picked up one of the two trodebands. If she was rattled by the rowdy scene around her, her steely expression betrayed no sign of it.

Dezmund leaned close to Maddox. "Your boy's in big trouble."

"It wouldn't be the first time."

Maddox watched as Tommy egged the crowd on, cupping his hand behind his ear and squinting like he could hardly hear them, like their cheers weren't nearly loud enough for someone of his awesome talent. The bar's customers responded, their chants growing louder as they clapped and whistled and stomped their feet. Tommy Park had the spotlight, and he was loving every moment of it. Maddox couldn't help but smile at the kid's bravado. It was an utterly misguided confidence, of course, but that didn't diminish its entertainment value. The kid was a born ham.

The contest rules were simple: two datajackers plugged into an offline digital environment, a simulated datasphere or some other purpose-built domain designed to test their skills. Once the clock started, whoever completed the designated task first was the winner. Most often, the objective was to find a simulated datasphere's vulnerability, exploit it, and steal some predetermined dataset. All without getting detected, of course. A short-range wireless broadcast allowed spectators to watch each avatar's perspective on their specs.

As the two datajackers readied themselves, adjusting their trodebands and firing up their decks, the crowd of onlookers donned their specs and toggled over to the broadcast feed. Maddox and Dezmund scrolled through a menu of DS simulations on a small holo monitor projected above the table, finally agreeing on a recent submission to the library by a game designer known for his tough, realistic creations.

The simulation was loaded into the shared environment, and a timer counted down on every pair of specs in the bar. When it reached five seconds, the crowd shouted out the numbers, each one louder than the last.

"THREE…TWO…ONE…GO!!!"

In less than a minute it was over. And it went pretty much as Maddox had expected.

The ham got schooled.

*   *   *

"I told you she was good," Dezmund said, still basking in the glow of his victory. He sipped his free shot of whiskey, savoring it a moment before swallowing.

"You didn't lie," Maddox said.

They sat alone in Maddox's small office in the back of the bar. Through the closed door came muffled tones of conversation and the low, thudding beat of technopop.

"So how's business?" Dezmund asked.

"Not bad. Not getting rich running a saloon, mind you, but I can't complain."

"I wasn't talking about your side hustle," Dezmund clarified.

"Ah," Maddox said, lighting a cigarette. "Same thing. No complaints."

"How many do you have on the payroll these days? It's not really just you and the kid, is it?"

Maddox blew smoke. "It is, actually. Just the two of us."

Dezmund shook his head as if he was disappointed to hear it. "Blackburn, Blackburn. You gotta think about the future. Our business is no different from any other. If you're not growing, you're dying."

"More crew means more headaches." Maddox shrugged. "And who needs that?"

Dezmund nodded in agreement. "Won't disagree with you there. You'd be amazed how much time I spend breaking up melodramas." He lifted the glass, finished off the whiskey. "Price of success, I suppose."

Maddox took a long drag, resisted the urge to roll

his eyes at the humble-bragging. Yes, yes, you're the big shot in the room, he was tempted to say. You have a bigger crew, you live on a higher floor, blah blah blah. Could this guy's dick be any smaller?

"Still," Dezmund went on, "maybe if you had a bigger crew you could quote more bids and not have to steal business from me."

Maddox blew smoke. He didn't bother to deny what they both knew was true. He had indeed won business by undercutting Dezmund, and he'd done it on more than one occasion. After he'd bought Winner Take Nothing and reopened its doors to the public, those first several months had been shaky ones, financially speaking. Running a bar was expensive, as Maddox had learned, and the place wasn't coming close to breaking even. Desperate for cash, Maddox lowballed a few deals, snatching them from Dezmund's grasp. More than a few deals, if he was being honest.

So, yes, the man sitting in front of him had every right to be righteously angry at his competitor, but at the moment, for whatever reason, he didn't appear to be.

"Just want you know I'm not here to give you hell about all that," Dezmund said, then added, "though I probably should."

"You seemed pretty pissed about it earlier," Maddox pointed out.

Dezmund shrugged. "Just playing to the crowd. Can't let my crew think I've gone soft, can I?"

"God forbid."

"I'm here about an opportunity, something we can both profit from. A once-in-a-lifetime job. I'm talking really good money, Blackburn."

"Interesting," Maddox said, though he wasn't moved. Every datajacker he'd ever known occasionally—and some more often than others—fell victim to a kind of criminal overoptimism. A misguided conviction that their next job would be the best one ever, the Big One, the impossibly lucrative windfall they'd been waiting for their entire crooked life. Even Maddox, sober and skeptical by nature, had fallen into the same trap once or twice, overestimating some gig's upside while looking past the downside.

"Why do you need my help?" Maddox asked. He lifted his chin toward the door. "Looks like you have plenty in-house talent."

"I do," Dezmund agreed. "They're very good. But this gig needs…specific experience."

"Meaning?"

"It's a brokerage house."

Maddox took a long, contemplative draw. "Which one?"

"BNO Commerz."

Maddox blew smoke and fought back the urge to laugh. There was overly ambitious, and then there was just plain stupid. For Maddox, the idea of robbing a company like BNO fit squarely into the latter category.

BNO Commerz was the largest financial brokerage firm in the world. And like every large global company involved in banking or investment trading, they spent billions on data security. Banks and brokerage firms and other financial institutions were in the trust business, and if customers were going to let them manage huge sums of their money, they needed to be one hundred percent sure there was zero possibility of some data thief sneaking in and emptying their accounts.

"You're joking," Maddox said.

"I'm not."

"Come on," Maddox scoffed. "BNO's a top-five bank. You know how tight they lock down their DSes. They spend a fortune to keep our dirty little hands out of their cookie jar. Those places have the biggest, meanest AIs around." Financial firms' dataspheres were the most secure, most impenetrable virtual environments that existed. Maddox had never heard of anyone breaching the DS of a top financial company like BNO. The very idea was lunacy. Like thinking you could break through a bank's vault door with a carpenter's hammer.

Dezmund sat there silently, a hint of a smile on his face. Then it hit Maddox.

"You've got an in," he said.

"I've got an in," Dezmund repeated.

That might make things different, Maddox reflected. Might.

"I'm listening," he said, tapping his cigarette over the ashtray.

Dezmund leaned forward. "I've had a plant in their data security department for a year."

"A plant?" Maddox said in disbelief. "How'd you get someone from your crew past an employment screen?"

"That's the beauty of it," Dezmund said. "We didn't have to clean her history at all. She came to us, right out of college. Zero criminal background. She just didn't want to work in the legit world. Wanted to run with a datajacking crew." He chuckled. "Kids today. Go figure."

"Sounds too good to be true."

"Exactly what I thought, until we checked her out. She was clean and pristine. Top grades, even. So I think to myself, what's the best way to use someone with a spotless record, right out of school with a degree in cybersecurity?"

"Plant her in a big firm," Maddox said, finishing the thought.

"Exactly. And she's spent the past year getting herself into a spot where she can help me." He leaned in closer. "Now, BNO announces its earning results in four days. And anyone who knows those results before they're public stands to clean up in the markets."

Maddox smoked thoughtfully as he listened. Stealing earnings results before they went public wasn't a new scam. Dealing in inside information had probably been around as long as publicly traded markets had. And while Maddox rarely invested in stocks and bonds—like most criminals, he preferred the liquidity of hard cash and cash-based accounts— he knew enough about the markets to be skeptical. He reminded Dezmund how government agencies had AIs watching for unusual buying and selling activity before earnings calls, and how highfloor traders and executives—people with far more market sophistication than datajackers—got busted all the time for insider trading.

"That's the beauty of it," Dezmund said. "I'm not going to buy or sell a single share. I've got a hedge fund manager on the line. I come through with the goods, he'll pay." He went on, explaining how he'd invested months setting the whole thing up. He'd profiled dozens of hedge fund managers, narrowing them down to a single potential customer: a Swiss national with the perfect mix of moral flexibility and an impeccable reputation.

Dezmund had carefully approached the fund manager, and once the man had been convinced the datajacker wasn't some scam artist, he'd seized the opportunity to earn an easy billion or two.

"I got the feeling," Dezmund said, "it wasn't the first time he'd dealt in inside info."

"Does he know who you are?" Maddox asked.

Dezmund gave him a disdainful look. "Please, Blackburn. You think I'd show my face on something this big?"

"People take risks when there's a lot of money involved."

"Well, I'm not one of them, and you ought to know that. Crooks like us don't make it this long in this business if we show our faces to the clients, do we? It was all set up with blind go-betweens and quantum-encrypted calls, same as always."

Maddox didn't sense Dezmund was lying. He reminded himself the man sitting across from him might be a strutting peacock who shamelessly basked in his infamy, but when it came down to business, he wasn't the kind to cut corners or take unnecessary risks. Dez was a top pro. Vain and show-offy as fuck, but still a top pro.

He gazed at Maddox for a long moment, as if he was trying to gauge his colleague's interest. "So are you in?"

A ribbon of bluish smoke rose from the tip of Maddox's cigarette. He couldn't deny he was intrigued. The man had done his homework, and it was clearly going to be a lucrative job.

Still, banks were risky. Life-and-death kind of

risky. Even if you had someone holding the door open for you or distracting the company's guard dog AI while you snuck in, there were still lots of other nasty defensive apps and countermeasures waiting to jump on you.

And then there was the obvious question, which Maddox went ahead and voiced.

"You've been setting this up for a year," he said. "Why bring me in at the eleventh hour?"

A sheepish look came over Dezmund's features. It was a rare crack in the man's unwavering confidence.

"This is the biggest job I've ever taken on," he admitted. "And I'd be lying if I told you I wasn't worried about it. You're the only one I know who's ever breached a bank or taken on an AI. And even though I've got my insider, it's still a bank, and I'd feel a lot better about things if I had you on the crew for this one."

Maddox turned it over. The bar wasn't an anchor around his neck anymore. The place was making money these days, though only by the thinnest of margins. He wasn't the desperate cash-strapped Maddox he'd been a few months ago. Still, the opportunist in him hated to let a big payday slip away.

"I don't know if I can take some teenager telling me what to do," he said.

"You don't have to worry about that," Dezmund said. "I'll keep them in line."

Maddox blew smoke. "I'll have to think about it."

Dezmund's features dropped in disappointment. "You'll have to think about it." He nodded slowly. "You do that, Blackburn. You think about it. And I'll think about whether or not I care about those jobs you stole from me."

Maddox winced inwardly. He had known at some point Dezmund would play that card, and he had no counter for it.

There were unwritten rules among datajackers. Things you did and didn't do. Undercutting a competitor once or twice, for example, was no big deal. Everybody did that kind of thing once in a while. But if you did it too often, and to the wrong party, you could end up in a trash dumpster with a bullet in your head. Maddox had assumed Dezmund's operation was so large, so lucrative, that the man wouldn't care about a few lost deals. But apparently he'd hitched a ride on Dezmund's coattails one too many times, and now he was expected to make amends, to repay the debt.

Maddox cursed himself for being lazy, for stealing deals instead of putting in the time and effort to drum up his own business. For giving Dezmund leverage over him. He could almost see Rooney shaking his head at him, telling him he'd made his bed, and now he had to sleep in it.

Mashing out his cigarette, he sighed. He owed the man sitting across from him. Whether he liked it or not.

"All right," he said. "I'm in."

3
HELLO, SALARYMAN

Well past midnight, Winner Take Nothing's throbbing technopop had been silenced, and the place had cleared out except for one last customer, drunk and passed out in a corner booth. The suited corporati, who'd apparently had two or three too many, snored deeply. The man's mouth gaped open and his cheek was pressed against the tabletop.

Sitting on a barstool, Maddox pondered what exactly he'd signed up for, debating whether or not he should try to get out of it. Dezmund had assured him there would be a nice payout, and for his efforts Maddox would receive a generous portion. He'd also made sure Maddox understood that helping with this job would balance the ledger between them. That whatever bad blood Maddox's deal-stealing had caused, all would be forgiven. Still, with all the upsides, Maddox couldn't help dwelling on the downsides. The risk to life and limb, the risk of getting busted. And beyond all that, there was something else, some intangible thing poking at his gut. Something about this job that felt wrong.

The unconscious corporati's snoring finally grew loud enough to interrupt Maddox's second-guessing. The datajacker lit a cigarette and gestured to Feng, the massive bouncer who was halfway through his closing duties, wiping down tables with a rag and a bottle of spray cleaner.

"Got it, boss," Feng said, setting down the bottle and tossing the rag over his shoulder. Maddox subvocalized a command in his specs, calling a cab to take the man home. Feng lifted the drunken man gingerly and half-walked, half-carried the suit to the front door. Someone from outside opened the door and held it for them, entering the bar after the pair exited.

"We're closed," Maddox said to the silhouette standing in the entryway. Whoever it was didn't move.

The datajacker swiveled away from the bar and slid off the stool. "I said we're closed," he called, a bit louder.

As the woman stepped forward out of the shadow, a smile touched Maddox's lips. Apparently, this was his night for surprise visitors.

"Hello, salaryman," Beatrice said.

END OF PREVIEW

Hope you enjoyed this snippet from THE BLAYZE WAR, the third book in the CYBERPUNK CITY series.

ACKNOWLEDGEMENTS

My sincerest thanks to my editors Holly Walrath and Eliza Dee, both a pleasure to work with.

Thanks also to Audie Wallbrink. The series is much better than it would have been without her invaluable feedback.

And I'm enormously grateful to Ignacio Bazan-Lazcano, the amazing artist who brought the world of my words to new heights with his unbelievable covers. Thanks, Ignacio!

ABOUT THE AUTHOR

D.L. Young is a Texas-based author. He's a Pushcart Prize nominee and winner of the Independent Press Award. His stories have appeared in many publications and anthologies.

For free books, new release updates, and exclusive previews, visit his website at www.dlyoungfiction.com.

Printed in Great Britain
by Amazon

32554757R00138